A Dog
on
Barkham Street

Mary Stolz

Pictures by Leonard Shortall

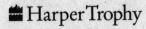
HarperTrophy

A Division of HarperCollinsPublishers

For Elizabeth Schaefer

CHAPTER
1

Edward Frost, who had his share of problems, didn't see how he'd ever solve the biggest one. This was Martin Hastings, the bully of Barkham Street. Martin was two years older than Edward, and there was no solution for this. Martin would continue to be two years older until he was a hundred and Edward was ninety-eight. Edward had a feeling that even then he might not be entirely safe.

The fact that he had only one enemy didn't help Edward much, because Martin lived next door to him. Edward lived at number 21 Barkham Street, and Martin lived at number 23. There was no solution for this, either. How could you avoid your enemy if every time you looked out a door he looked out a window and saw you?

"Why doesn't Dad get a job in Alaska, now that it's a state?" Edward asked his mother one day.

Mrs. Frost didn't look surprised at the question,

but she said Edward's father couldn't very well change his job just like that. Mr. Frost was a teacher at a university in St. Louis.

"Alaska would be fun," Edward insisted, without much hope. "I'll bet there's a lot of room for teachers up there. I bet they need them badly. You'd think Dad would want to go where he was needed."

Mrs. Frost sighed. "Is it Martin Hastings again?" she said.

Edward nodded.

"What did he do this time?"

This time Martin had chased him for blocks, and then, when Edward was absolutely exhausted and fell down, Martin sat on top of him and pulled his hair and said over and over, "Uncle, say *uncle*. . . ."

Martin was a big boy, and Edward not especially. It was an awful, grinding feeling to be sat on that way. And though Martin hadn't pulled hard it was terrible to have your hair pulled at all.

Edward had held out as long as he could, and then gasped, "Uncle," and was released. He got up shakily, dusted off his trousers, and walked away with Martin's voice loud in his ears.

"Don't forget, now," Martin yelled. "Whenever I look at you and wiggle my finger, you gotta say uncle. Understand, Weird One?"

Edward kept walking, not too fast, because that might start everything all over again, but without answering or looking back. He hated being called Weird One almost as much as he hated the pounding, but there was nothing he could do about that either.

There was no point in telling his mother all this, because it didn't so much matter what Martin did or said, it was just the fact that Martin was there, big and mean and living next door. It was the fact that Edward, looking ahead, could see no way in which any of this would be changed, unless Martin moved away or dropped dead. Neither seemed likely.

"I'm going to get a crew cut," he said now.

"That's fine," said his mother.

"I think I'll take a course in muscle-building, too. I'll write to one of those magazines about how you get your muscles like cannonballs, and then I'll poke him in the jaw and knock him out for a week and when he comes to I'll make him say uncle for a month without stopping."

"You can't do that. I mean, you can't take a strong-man course."

"Why not?"

"Because your muscles aren't developed yet."

"That's exactly what *I'm* saying," Edward pointed out. "I'm going to—"

"No," said his mother. "What I mean is, you aren't old enough for weight lifting and all that sort of thing. You have to be—oh, well into your teens before you can do such things."

"How well into them?"

"Fourteen, anyway, I should think."

"Oh, crums," said Edward in a gloomy voice.

Fourteen seemed practically as far away as ninety-eight. Maybe he should concentrate on learning to run fast. He supposed it was cowardly to run, but the sight of Martin looming around corners like a bear always got his legs into action before he had time to think. And if he *had* to run, the smart thing would be to run fast enough not to get caught.

"You know," his mother was saying, "even if we did move somewhere else, it wouldn't be much help, probably. I understand there's a bully on every block. I expect even Alaskan blocks. It's what the other mothers tell me, at PTA meetings, and all."

"What do the mothers of the bullies say?"

Mrs. Frost shook her head. "I guess maybe they often don't know. Martin Hastings' mother doesn't know. Or won't believe it. Nobody can tell her anything."

"I heard Ruth Ann's mother telling her one day. Ruth Ann's mother said Martin ought to be locked in an attic until he comes of age."

"Oh, but that's a dreadful thing to say."

"You know what he did? Ruth Ann and some girls were making a tea party for dolls in the back yard, and Martin went in and knocked everything over, except he drank the ginger ale—that was the tea."

Mrs. Frost looked unhappy. "Well, it was a bad thing to do."

"Ruth Ann's mother and Mrs. Hastings yelled at each other all over the place. Didn't you hear them?"

"I must have been away, thank heaven. Edward, *I* don't know what the answer is. But I'm just glad you aren't a bully."

Edward snorted. "Me? I'm the kind who runs."

"What else can you do? You needn't be ashamed of running if there's nothing else to do."

"Dad says I should stand up to him."

"How can you stand up to somebody twice your size?"

"Dunno," said Edward. But secretly, while liking his mother for understanding how hard it all

6

was, he sort of agreed with his father. The trouble was that in order to stand up to somebody you had to remember to stand still, and he always forgot and ran. It was a problem, all right.

"I'm going over to Rod's house now," he told his mother. "We're going to finish our birdhouses today."

"Good. Are you taking your bike?"

"Yes."

"Well, watch out for cars. And be home by five o'clock."

"All right," said Edward, pulling on his jacket. He went out to the garage, where he kept his bike. As he rode he looked around for Martin, and was relieved to see no sign of him.

Edward was glad he was going to have his wren house finished today, because he wanted to get it hanging before the wrens came and all found somewhere else to live. He and Rod had been working for a week in Rod's father's workshop. Today they'd paint their houses, and then all that remained was to hang them up and wait for the wrens to arrive.

Rod was sitting on his front porch steps, eating some raw potato, when Edward pulled into the driveway and parked on the edge of it.

"Hi," said Edward loudly.

7

Rod came toward him in a hurry. "We have to be quiet," he warned.

"Oh, okay. Why?"

"My sister's going to the hospital to have a new baby and she's left the old one with us. He's asleep."

"You mean you're *two* uncles," Edward exclaimed.

"Going to be," Rod said modestly. "When the next one gets born, of course."

Edward was enormously impressed. He was almost as enormously jealous. It seemed too much for Rod to be able to go around talking about two nephews. One had been bad enough. Rod was the only person their age Edward knew who was an uncle at all.

"So now you're going to have two nephews," he said, trying to sound pleasant.

"Well . . . it might be a girl. That'd be a niece."

This made it a little better, but not much.

"I can think of something I'd rather have than a nephew, or a niece," Rod said.

Edward nodded. He could, too. Both he and Rod would rather have had a dog.

"But the thing is," Edward pointed out, "I don't have either one. No dog. And no nephew."

Since this was plainly the truth, Rod said nothing. He offered Edward a piece of potato, and they went into the house and started for the basement workshop.

"Hello, Edward," said Mrs. Graham, coming out of the kitchen. "Try to be quiet, won't you, boys?"

"I've already told him," Rod said.

"I hope your daughter has a nice baby," Edward said.

Mrs. Graham laughed happily. "So do we, Edward, so do we."

"Rod's pretty lucky, being an uncle all the time this way."

"Isn't he?"

"I still wish I had a dog," Rod said quickly.

Edward nodded to himself. Rod was pretty good about picking times to ask for a dog. Here his mother was in such a good mood about the babies, and all. Who could tell what she might agree to? But the answer, when it came, was the same as always. It was the same one his own mother gave whenever he brought up the subject of a dog, which was often.

"Rod, dear," said Mrs. Graham. "Haven't you understood yet that your father and I do not think you should have a dog until you're old enough to take responsibility?"

"How do you know I'm not old enough now?" Rod asked.

Edward didn't need to listen to know what the answer to that was.

"When you're old enough to do the few jobs we give you now, Rod, such as tidying up your room, or running an errand now and then without complaining, then we'll consider it. Every single mother I've talked to who's gotten a dog for a child your age has wound up taking care of it herself. The boys *say* they will, and *swear* they will, but, once the novelty is over, who's left to do it? The mothers. No thank you, dear. I have enough to do now."

Rod sighed. "Okay. Just thought I'd ask. Let's go, Edward."

They went down to the workshop, but did not immediately get at the painting of the wren houses.

"You know," Rod said, sitting on a wooden stool and scowling at the floor, "I'd sure like to get ahold of the guys around here who got dogs and then didn't take care of them. I'd paste their ears back."

Edward agreed that it was that sort of boy who made trouble for boys like him and Rod, who would *certainly* take care of their dogs if they could get them.

Martin Hastings had been given a dog for his last birthday, but after a week he'd started forgetting to come home after school to take it for a run (you weren't supposed to let dogs loose in this town), refusing to get up early to feed and take it out, and generally leaving everything for his mother to do. After three weeks the dog had mysteriously disappeared. Martin had carried on something awful, but he didn't get the dog back. A pain in the neck, no matter how you looked at him, that Martin Hastings. Still, Edward couldn't offer to paste those ears back, so he said, "We'd take care of our dogs."

"Boy," said Rod. "I'd get mine a rope about four times as long as a regular leash, and I'd get up at five o'clock every morning and run with him for miles—"

"Five o'clock!" Edward protested. "Not me. My dog's going to have to wait till . . . oh, till six-thirty, or so. But I'll give him a long rope and a long run. And I'll remember to feed him, and I'll take him with me when I go biking—"

"Take who with you?" Rod interrupted.

"My dog, of course. What are we talking about?"

"What dog?"

Edward lapsed into silence for a while, and then said, "Maybe we ought to start straightening up our rooms, or running errands or something. Do you think maybe then they'd really give us a dog?"

Rod shrugged. "Besides," he said, not very certainly, "I do straighten my room. Sort of. Could be better on errands, I suppose."

"So do I. Sort of." Edward remembered that today, when he'd changed his jeans and his old shirt, he'd left his school clothes lying around somewhere. He hoped it was on the bed and not on the floor. But only yesterday he'd bicycled down to the store for bread. Of course, on the way home he'd accidentally dropped it and his back wheel had run over it slightly, but most of the loaf had been all right. Even so, his mother had said he was just plain careless.

"I don't think I'm anywhere near getting a dog yet," he said.

"Me either," said Rod.

They sighed and were silent for a while, and then Rod got up and walked slowly to the paint cans. "We've got blue and yellow and black," he said. "What color you want?"

"Yellow," said Edward.

The next afternoon Edward was up in the back-yard beech tree, hanging his yellow wren house, when Martin came out of his side door, slamming it behind him. He stood on the stoop, turning his head from side to side.

Looking around for trouble, Edward thought, and stayed very still. He felt like an animal pro-tecting itself with camouflage. Except that he really didn't think he blended cunningly with a silver-gray beech that had only the smallest leaves on it. He wore a black and red plaid shirt and blue jeans. All Martin had to do was to look his way.

However, Martin did not. He sauntered off down the street. Edward finished adjusting his birdhouse, climbed down, and stood looking up at it. It rocked gently and turned a little from side to side. Edward could not see how a pair of wrens could resist it. He'd gotten it up in time, too, be-cause he hadn't seen a sign of a wren yet this year.

"That's lovely, Edward," said his mother, open-ing a window in the kitchen. "It looks simply beau-tiful."

"Doesn't it?" said Edward. "Don't you think the first wrens who see it will move in?"

"They'd be pretty silly not to."

"That's what I thought," Edward said, still look-ing up in the branches of the tree.

He heard the kitchen window close, because it was still not warm enough to leave windows open this late in the day, and then he heard another sound behind him, but before he could identify it he was flat on the ground. The grassy earth was soft, so he wasn't hurt, but as he rolled around he was so filled with rage that tears sprang from his eyes. For a second, he really thought he'd go for Martin, who had sneaked back so quietly and pushed him while his back was turned. He thought that this time his anger would pitch him into battle before he'd had time to think. And even though he'd be sure to lose the fight, he would at least have tried.

But it was already too late, because he'd already thought. He scrambled to his feet and stood panting, facing a laughing Martin who wiggled his finger and waited, wiggled his finger again.

"I will not," Edward said breathlessly.

"Sure you will," said Martin. He wiggled his finger again and moved forward a step.

"What are you making there, Weird One?"

Knowing it would make things worse, but not able to help himself, Edward said, "It's a trap to catch fat boys. Better stay out of the trees, Martin."

Martin started for him angrily, and Edward,

scared now, opened his mouth to say the hated, demanded word. *Uncle*, he was just about to say, when his mother's voice called, "Edward, will you come here a moment, please."

"Say it," Martin warned.

But Edward ducked and ran around him, and ran into his house, to his mother. He was so angry at having done this that he burst into tears, and that made him even angrier. At Martin, at himself, and at his mother, too.

"You did that on purpose, didn't you?" he said, blowing his nose loudly. "You called me so Martin would know you were around."

"Well . . . yes," said Mrs. Frost. "I just looked out and saw the two of you and . . . it seemed like a good idea."

"Well, it was, I suppose," Edward admitted. "Only that's the *trouble*, don't you see?"

"I see quite well. What I don't see is what else I could do. Stand at the window and watch him beat you up?"

"Someday," said Edward, "oh, *someday*, I'm going to paste his ears back."

Mrs. Frost looked out the window at the wren house in the beech tree. "That looks very inviting," she said. "I'm sure the wrens will love it."

Edward had to agree that it did look fine, bobbing gently among the thin young leaves. But somehow he wasn't very interested in it any more. It was getting so he couldn't be interested in anything for very long—not even dogs—because the problem of Martin was always in the way.

CHAPTER

2

Edward stood at the window and watched the rain tossing in sudden gusts along the street when the wind caught it, then falling straight again. Once in a while a car went by, its tires hissing, and once a wet, ruffled robin bounded across the grass and then took to its wings and flew, apparently, over the roof.

Now a dog came running along, its nose to the ground, its back quite sleek with water. Edward watched it hopefully. There were no end of stories in which the boy wanted a dog but didn't get one until a wonderful dog came along and selected *him*. In the stories these dogs were either stray ones, or the people who owned them saw how the boy and the dog loved each other and gave the dog up.

In the stories the parents agreed to keep the dog, even if they'd been very much against the idea before.

Edward was always looking around for some dog that would follow him home from school and refuse to leave. In a case like that, he didn't see how his mother could refuse. He had even, a couple of times, tried to lure a dog to follow him. Whistling at it, snapping his fingers, running in a tempting way. But he must have picked dogs that already had homes and liked them. Now if this dog, this wet dog running along by itself in the rain, should suddenly stop at his house, and come up to the door and cry to be let in . . . wouldn't his mother be *sure* to let Edward have him? You couldn't leave a dog out in the rain, could you? The dog ran across the street, ran back, dashed halfway over the lawn, stopped to shove its nose in a puddling flowerpot, backed off sneezing, sat down and scratched its chin.

Edward held his breath, waiting. After a moment he tapped lightly on the windowpane. The dog cocked its head in an asking gesture, got to its feet, then wheeled around and continued down the street. Edward sighed. He was not at all surprised—the dog had a collar with at least four license tags dangling from it—but still he sighed. He was pretty sure he'd forgotten to make his bed and suspected that a hammer he'd been using yesterday was now lying in the back yard getting pretty wet. Mr. Frost was particular about his tools, and Edward felt that dogs, if they weren't getting further away from him, certainly weren't coming any nearer. He decided to go up and make his bed. He didn't see what there was to do about the hammer just now, since his mother would notice if he went out in the rain to get it.

The mailman turned the corner, and Edward lingered to watch him. Mr. Dudley had his mail sack and a tremendous black umbrella to juggle. He wore a black slicker that glistened in the rain and shining mud-splashed rubbers and a plastic cover on his hat. He was late already but he moved slowly, as if he were tired.

"Mr. Dudley's coming," Edward said, as his mother came in the room.

Mrs. Frost came over to the window. "Poor man," she said. "Stay and ask him if he'd like to come in for a cup of coffee."

Edward waited, and when Mr. Dudley turned up their walk, he ran to the front door and opened it. "Mother says do you want some coffee, Mr. Dudley," he asked, as he took the mail.

"Well now, that's a handsome offer," Mr. Dudley said, frowning down at his rubbers, "but does your mother know I'm just this side of drowned?"

"Oh, that's all right," Edward said cheerfully. "You take off your rubbers and raincoat here on the porch."

Mr. Dudley laid down the mail sack and his huge black umbrella. "Can't say a cup of coffee won't be welcome," he observed, as he and Edward made for the kitchen.

Mrs. Frost gave the mailman a sweet bun with his coffee, and Edward a cup of cocoa. They sat in the breakfast nook and the rain beat against the window, making things quite snug. Edward glanced out in the back yard. There was the hammer, all right. In perfectly plain view. He guessed his mother hadn't noticed it yet, and decided that rain or no rain he was going to have to go after it. It was too good a hammer to leave there until his father got home and saw it.

"Notice you have a letter there from Arizona, Mrs. Frost," said Mr. Dudley. He licked the sugar daintily from his fingers and Edward watched with admiring envy. He wondered if Mr. Dudley's mother had told him, when he was a little boy, "Don't lick your fingers, dear, use the napkin." He decided she probably had and now Mr. Dudley, all grown up, was doing as he pleased. It was satisfying to watch and look forward to. Edward was really looking forward to growing up. And the first thing I'll do, he said to himself now, is move to some city that Martin Hastings never heard of.

Mrs. Frost had picked up the letter from Arizona. Her forehead wrinkled the way it did when a pie came out of the oven not looking as she'd planned it to. Edward and Mr. Dudley waited for her to say who it was from. Or, perhaps, "How strange—who can it be from?" Or, "So it is—a letter from Arizona." But she said none of these things. She frowned at the letter, and then, in a funny gesture, put the other letters on top of it, and asked Mr. Dudley if he wanted another cup of coffee.

After the mailman had gone, Edward began to say, "Who is that letter from—" but his mother interrupted him. This was something she practically never did, since she was always telling Edward how he shouldn't, and it made him begin to be very curious about the letter. His mother asked if he'd made his bed and he said maybe he ought to go up and see, so he climbed the stairs to his room, wondering all the way (about the letter, not the bed), and found that sure enough everything was rumpled and tossed around just as he had left it.

Suddenly, because that possible dog was on his mind, and because there was nothing else to do,

Edward decided to make a tremendous gesture. He would clean his entire room. He would stack the books that lay around so carelessly. He would straighten his toys and his clothes. He'd get out the vacuum and do the rug. Maybe he'd even clean the closet. Yes, that was a great idea. He'd never cleaned the closet in his life. His mother would be so bowled over she'd probably offer him a St. Bernard on the spot.

He plunged in at once, dragging out clothes, books, fishing equipment, old forgotten trucks and games. He put the clothes on the still-unmade bed, shoved everything else out on the floor. It seemed to take an awfully long time to get the closet emptied, and then when he thought he was done he looked up, saw the shelves, and wished he'd never started.

They were absolutely jammed with junk. Well, maybe it wasn't all junk, but it looked it. And now his room was filled to brimming with things that would have to be put away again. He sat on his heels and stared around, thinking that the whole idea of cleaning up was pretty silly. Everything was just going to have to be put back in the closet, so what was the point of taking it out in the first place?

"My word, Edward," said his mother at the door, "what are you doing?"

"Cleaning my room," he said glumly.

"That's a good idea," she said, coming in. "Did all that come out of the closet?"

Edward nodded. "And it all has to go back," he said. "And I was just thinking, what's the point? I mean, where do you get *ahead*? I don't think I'll clean it after all."

"You can't leave it this way," said Mrs. Frost. She picked up a battered green dump truck. "Do you ever use this?" When Edward said he didn't suppose so, at least he hadn't in a long time, she said, "Why don't you get a box from the cellar and put the things you don't really want in it, and we'll give it to the Salvation Army? They're marvelous at fixing things up for Christmas. It seems to me there must be a lot of things you've outgrown. When you get all that sorted out, you won't have so much to put back, and you'll be neater, *and* ahead. Sweep the closet out before you put your things away, of course, and put them away tidily. I see you hadn't made your bed after all."

There was no reasonable answer to this, so Edward stumped down to the basement for a box, wondering if dogs appreciated what people had to

go through to get them. He paused at the cellar door, looking out. The rain hadn't slackened any. Or had it? He leaned forward, pressing his nose to the glass. He wasn't fifteen feet from that hammer, and his mother was busy upstairs, so if he just dashed out . . .

Pulling his sweater up so that it partly covered his head, he opened the door and dashed. The grass was sopping, the earth beneath it marshy, and, though he got the hammer all right, his shoulders and feet were drenched even in so short a run. Back in the cellar, he dried the hammer thoughtfully and stared at his shoes. Finally he removed them. The socks were dry enough. He took a towel from the hamper and rubbed his head and the sweater. Picking up the box, he went upstairs in his stocking feet, hoping his mother wouldn't notice anything.

"Here's the box," he said in a loud cheerful voice. "Think it's big enough?"

His mother had her back to him. She was on a chair, getting things down from the shelves. "I thought," she said, not turning around yet, "that I'd help you out a little. This is really quite a big job. Here, you take these things, and I'll hand you down some more—" She glanced around and stopped talking. Her eyes went from his head to his feet.

"I suppose," she said, "you had some reason for going out in the pouring rain? Aside from its nuisance value, that is?"

Edward wiggled his shoulders. He disliked that kind of remark, and would have preferred to have her come right out and ask what the heck he thought he was doing. But just saying something right out was a thing grownups rarely did. In this, as in so many matters concerning adults, Edward failed to see the reason but accepted the fact.

"Somebody had left the hammer out in the rain," he mumbled. "It might've got rusty."

"Somebody?" said Mrs. Frost, lifting one eyebrow.

Edward debated, and then said with inspiration, "Well, *I'm* somebody, aren't I?"

Mrs. Frost began to scowl, looked at the ceiling, half-smiled, turned back to the closet, and said, "How about all these jigsaw puzzles?"

"They're a bit on the simple side," said Edward. He almost added that they could get him some harder ones, but decided this wasn't the best time for requests of any sort. His mother was being very nice about the rain and the hammer, so there was no point in annoying her.

It was a funny thing, he mused, piling things in the box for the Salvation Army, that lots of times he asked for things not really much wanting them at all. For instance, jigsaw puzzles. He didn't actually want any, he didn't even like doing them very much when he got them, but the habit of *asking* was just one he sort of had. He asked for Good Humors if the Good Humor man happened to be around, clothes if he happened to be in a store where they sold them, toys if he happened to see them in an advertisement or a shop window. He guessed that one way and another he asked for something or other every single day whether he wanted it or not. Sometimes he got the thing and sometimes he didn't, but anyone could see that the asking annoyed parents. Rod said he'd found that, too. Once Mr. Frost had said, "Edward, don't you ever bore yourself with these constant requests?" and Edward had said he didn't think so.

Still, thinking it over now, he wondered if it wouldn't be wiser to limit all the asking to a dog. If he concentrated on that, one of several things might happen. Either he'd wear them down so that at last they'd give in, or he'd impress them so much with how he wanted a dog and nothing else that they'd give in, or they'd get to be so sorry for him that they'd give in. Or—he had to admit—they'd get so irritated that he'd never see a dog until he was grown up himself. He piled a fleet of little trucks in the box, and sat back on his heels to think.

"Problems?" said his mother, coming away from the closet to inspect the box. Edward nodded. "Could I help?" Mrs. Frost asked.

"Probably not," he said sadly. Then he looked up and met his mother's blue, friendly eyes. "*How* responsible do I have to be before I can have a dog?"

"Quite a bit, I'm afraid. Now, Edward . . . look at today. Bed unmade again, hammer out in the rain, *you* out in the rain—"

"But I'm cleaning my whole room," he protested.

"You started to," his mother reminded him. "If you recall, you got everything out and then changed your mind."

"When I grow up," Edward said, "my boy will have a dog as soon as he asks for it. In fact, I bet having the dog will *teach* him to be responsible," he added hopefully.

"But suppose it doesn't? Suppose you get the dog, and he doesn't take care of it at all?"

"I wouldn't mind taking care of it myself."

"Well, that's where you and I differ," said Mrs. Frost. "I would mind."

Edward, realizing that he hadn't handled his end of the argument well at all, gave up for the time being.

So now he could either get on with the room because he'd started and ought to finish, or he could get on with it because his mother was perfectly sure to make him. He decided on the former, and, in as responsible a voice as he could manage, he said, "Guess I might as well finish up here, eh?"

"I guess you might as well," said Mrs. Frost with a smile. "I'll have to leave you. I'm making a lemon meringue pie."

"You are?" said Edward with pleasure. There were few things he preferred to lemon meringue pie. "Gee, that's great." He went and fetched the vacuum cleaner and set to work in a good humor, the matter of dogs dwindling to the back of his mind.

Even people who wanted something badly couldn't think about it every single minute.

In the evening, after dinner, the Frosts were sitting in the living room, relaxing. Mr. Frost read his paper, Mrs. Frost her book, and Edward, who had used up his hour of television long ago, lay on the floor with his feet on a chair wondering why the good guys *always* beat the bad guys. It couldn't be that way in real life.

"Dad?" he said, tilting his head back so he could look at his father upside down.

"Hmm?" said Mr. Frost. He peered over the top of his newspaper. "Hmm?"

"If you were caught in a burning barn, with ten men outside all blazing away at you with six-shooters and you had only one bullet and a broken leg, what would you do?"

"Burn up or get shot, I suppose. Do I have a choice?"

"Why wouldn't you leap on the horse and ride out the back door to get the posse?"

"I thought my leg was broken?"

"This horse would understand. He'd get in a position to make it easy for you."

"I can't ride a horse no matter what position he's in."

Edward laughed. "Then you wouldn't win out against all the odds?"

"I'm afraid not. But then I'm not an actor."

Edward twisted around and sat up. "But it can't be only actors who win out against all the odds. How about somebody, say, who wants something *badly* and everybody says no you can't, but this person struggles and tries—and persists. How about that? Couldn't he win in the end?"

"If this person paid attention to a few simple things he'd been asked to do," Mrs. Frost said, "I daresay he'd win in the end."

"This person is trying," said Edward, lying down again.

"Not very hard," said his mother. "For instance, weren't you going to remember by yourself when it was time to get ready for bed? You said if I didn't tell you, you'd remember better and do it without fussing. Well, I haven't reminded you, and now it's nearly an hour past your bedtime. I've been wondering when you were going to remember.

This is just one example, mind you. There are others."

Edward got to his feet, feeling somehow that he'd been taken advantage of. Yet the fact remained that he *had* said he'd remember and he'd gone and forgotten nearly every night this week. "When I get to be a parent," he warned them, "I'm never going to remind my children of *any*thing."

"Then remind me not to visit you," said Mr. Frost. "Except perhaps at Christmas."

"Now be sure you take a bath," said Mrs. Frost. "Don't forget your ears."

Edward trailed out of the room and started upstairs, pulling himself up by the banister, step after slow step. When he got to the landing, he stopped and ran his hand three times around the newel post. He did this every night for luck. On the third round, he heard his mother's voice say, "Ed? I had a letter from my brother today."

"Oh?" said Mr. Frost. "Good. How's the old boy doing? Where is he?"

"He's in Arizona. He says he's been working in a hotel in the Grand Canyon National Park. And I guess he's all right. He's going to pay us a visit."

"Well, that's great."

"Great?" said Mrs. Frost, her voice lifting a

little. "Do you realize that my brother is a . . . is a *tramp?*"

"Hobo," said Mr. Frost. "You don't really think he's a tramp. You're just saying that."

"Tramp, hobo . . . what's the difference?"

"There's a good deal of difference," said Mr. Frost, in his explaining tone that Edward knew so well. "A tramp is . . . well, a bum. A fellow who never works and usually hangs around cadging handouts. A hobo is a respectable person who just doesn't want to settle down. Josh is a gentleman of the road, and I'll be honored to have him visit us."

"You're making it sound as if I don't want to see him, and that isn't so. He's my brother and I love him. But I can't help wondering what sort of effect a . . . a hobo uncle will have on Edward."

Uncle Josh, Edward said in his mind. Uncle Josh. He had heard of this uncle, but in the vaguest way. Sometimes his mother said Edward was "exactly like Josh," and when Edward had inquired curiously who was the Josh he was just like, his mother said, "My brother. My older brother."

"Where is he?" Edward had asked.

"Heaven knows. But wherever he is, he's fine, I'm sure of that," Mrs. Frost had replied, and then somehow they'd always gotten off the subject.

Edward, listening on the landing, knew quite well that he was eavesdropping and that it was discouraged and considered impolite. This had always seemed to him quite unreasonable, as grown-ups rarely said anything interesting when they knew you could hear.

Now he heard his mother say, "That bathtub hasn't been run, has it? What in the world is he doing now, do you suppose?"

"Taking off a sock, probably. I remember I could start removing my shoes and socks and get to thinking about something and sit with a sock half off for hours. Or until my mother called me, of course."

"I think it's a shame that it's always mothers who have to do the calling. Fathers can show this grand understanding of how you can go into a dream over a sock, but *mothers* have to remind you that it's getting late, and that it's a school day tomorrow, and that if you don't get to sleep now you'll never get up in the morning. And who has to do the waking up in the morning, I ask you?"

"Mothers," said Mr. Frost brightly.

Edward sped to his room and whipped off his clothes. He was on his way to the bathroom to run the tub when his mother came upstairs.

"You practically haven't started," she accused her son.

"I'm hurrying," Edward said, looking at her tenderly. It was a shame that she always had to do the calling and reminding. He hadn't thought of it before. "I was just on my way."

"Be sure you soap behind your ears."

Edward stopped feeling tender. "Mother," he said, in a firm, patient voice, "this isn't my night for soap."

"What do you mean?" she said. "It isn't your night for *soap*? Every night is a night for soap. Soap goes with the bath."

"Not with mine it doesn't," Edward explained. "One night soap. Next night no soap. Why do I have to take a bath every night, anyway?"

"Well, dear, I could ask you the same question. Why do you?"

"Because you're bigger than I am, I suppose."

"Oh, *Edward*," said Mrs. Frost. She sighed. "Whatever am I going to do with you?"

"It's a problem," he admitted. "When's Uncle Josh coming?"

"You were eavesdropping," said his mother sternly.

"Sometimes I got to. When is he?"

"You never, never have to eavesdrop," said his mother.

"Uncle Josh wrote that letter from Arizona, didn't he?"

Mrs. Frost hesitated, and Edward waited rather warily. This was an important moment—the sort of moment that came from time to time, when his mother could go either of two ways. If she was awfully tired and had had a bad day and Edward had been especially exasperating, she might snap at him and tell him to get busy at what he'd been told to do. On the other hand, she might just relax and laugh. This was what she chose to do tonight.

"Oh, for goodness' sakes," she said. "Skip the bath. Wash up and get in bed and call me when you're ready. I'll *tell* you about your Uncle Josh. Hop to it."

Edward hopped to it.

When he was cozily in bed, his knees drawn up and his chin resting on them, his mother sat in the old chair that he had seen her in so many evenings of his life. In the days when he was read to at night, it was that chair she sat in with the book. Sometimes his father had read, but most often his mother. Now, of course, he read to himself. Nights when he'd had nightmares—which he didn't have any more but which had been very bad when he was younger—it was in that chair he and his mother had sat and talked softly, or sung to each other. His mother always said that a song in the night was good for chasing nightmares, and it had seemed to be so. When he was sick, the doctor put his bag on that chair before he turned and said, "Well, young man, let's have a look at you," and visitors sat there telling him how nice it was outdoors and what he was missing—or how awful it was and how he ought to feel lucky. The chair these days was usually piled with clothes and baseballs and books and things he couldn't decide what to do with, but tonight, of course, with his room all cleaned, it was neat and empty.

Now Mrs. Frost sat there and smiled at Edward, who smiled back and thought she looked nice. Sort of fussy and plump. Once again he felt sorry for her, that she should be the one who always had to do the reminding. "You know," he told her, "I guess it really isn't easy for mothers."

"Easy?" said Mrs. Frost in a surprised voice. "Easy how?"

"Always having to tell people to get up, and clean up, and hurry up. You know. Even Dad. I mean, you even have to tell him." It was true, his father was a very hard man to get up in the morning, and Mrs. Frost was always having to tell him that he'd be late for work if he didn't hurry. Secretly, Edward thought it would be easier all around if his mother stopped reminding everybody and let people take their chance on being late.

"Why," he said suddenly, "don't you just stop?"

"Stop telling you and your father things, you mean?"

Edward nodded.

Mrs. Frost thought for a minute. "I guess that would be even harder. Here all week I haven't been telling you when to go to bed, so you just haven't gone. And if I didn't ask you to make your bed, it wouldn't be made from one end of the week to the next, now would it?"

"Can't tell," said Edward. "It might."

"Furthermore, I honestly think your father would just *stay* in bed, if I didn't call him. You're both so much like Josh it's uncanny. Especially as your father isn't related to him at all. Laziness is catching."

"Is Uncle Josh lazy?"

Mrs. Frost looked a little embarrassed. "Well, no. Not really, I suppose. But he certainly isn't like other people."

"What *is* he like?"

"Like?" Edward's mother looked at the ceiling, as if she saw there a picture of her brother and was trying to describe it. "Like the Mole," she said at last.

Edward nodded. The Mole, of course. Mole, from the *Wind in the Willows*, which was about Edward's favorite book. Mole, one day in the middle of his spring housecleaning, had simply bolted without a backward glance and had gone forth to lead a carefree life in the sunshine.

"But Mole never *really* ran away," he pointed out. "He went back to his house once in a while. Remember how it kept calling to him? Does Uncle Josh have a house that keeps calling to him?"

"Well, no. Maybe he's more like Ratty. Ratty never did anything in particular, did he? And didn't care if he did?"

"But Ratty had his house, too. He never went past the Wild Wood to the Wide World. He stayed pretty much on the River, remember?"

"Not as well as you do, that's clear. Well, maybe he's like Toad. *He* certainly got out in the Wide World. Yes, like Toad. Sort of dashing and devil-may-care."

"But Toad was a problem to all his friends. Is Uncle Josh a problem?"

Mrs. Frost decided that the picture on the ceiling wasn't proving very accurate. She transferred her gaze to her son and said, "Let's say that your Uncle Josh is a bit like all wanderers and adventurers. He ran away from home, he doesn't much care if he gets anything in particular accomplished, and once in a while he *is* a problem to his friends. To his sister, anyway. I worry about him. If your own brother drifts about like a bit of tumbleweed and you almost never know where he is, you worry."

"And now you're worried about what sort of effect he'll have on me, being a hobo and all?"

"Don't use that *word*," Mrs. Frost said loudly. "And stop listening to conversations that don't concern you. I warn you, Edward, this eavesdropping is going to get you in trouble. Someday you'll hear something you're really *not* meant to hear. Eavesdroppers are not only rude, they often get badly hurt."

Edward didn't agree, so he said nothing except, "Dad called Uncle Josh a hobo. Why can't I?"

"Because."

Edward waited.

"Because people put different interpretations on a word like hobo. To your father it's romantic and carefree. But most people think it means a—a tramp. I don't think you want to go around giving people the impression that your uncle is a tramp, do you?"

"Oh, no."

"He's . . . a traveler. That's a better word. And it's true, too. He's been traveling for years and years. Ever since he was a boy."

"Didn't he go to school?"

"Yes, he went to school." Mrs. Frost sounded suddenly weary. "Until he was fifteen or sixteen, I think. Then one day he just went off. He started his—travels. And he's never stopped. It's a shame."

To Edward it sounded glorious. "Didn't he ever visit us before?"

"Once, when you were a baby. He arrived with a pony and a cart. That was how he was making a little money just then, giving children rides in the pony cart. We put them up in the garage. Not your uncle. The pony and cart. And all the ladies on the block were *too* kind to me, pretending it wasn't humiliating in the *least*."

"Was it?" said Edward, surprised.

"It was to me," Mrs. Frost replied grimly. "Very."

"That's a shame," said Edward. He added hope-

43

fully, "Does he still have them? I mean, will he bring—"

"No," said Mrs. Frost quickly. "He was only using them, or taking care of them, or whatever he was doing with them, while the man who really owned them was in the hospital having an operation. Josh has odd ways of making money, and I think he sees to it that he never makes very much."

"Why?"

"He doesn't believe in having things."

"He had a pony," Edward said enviously.

"Not for long."

"How else does he make a little money?"

Mrs. Frost hesitated, shrugged a little, and then said, "Let's let him tell you, shall we? He'll be here soon." She got up. "And now that we've made you hopelessly late in getting to sleep, I suppose I'll have to drag you out by your feet in the morning."

Edward grinned. "Maybe not."

He went to sleep almost immediately, and in the morning he was up even before his mother called. The coming of his Uncle Josh affected him the way Christmas did, and he couldn't have slept late if he'd been asked. Like Christmas, you weren't sure what the day would bring, but you knew it would be wonderful and strange.

44

CHAPTER

4

However, his Uncle Josh did not arrive that day, nor the day after, nor the day after that. Presently Edward began to think of other things.

Spring vacation was coming, and his class—as well as all the others—was preparing a skit for the preholiday assembly, which was to be held at night, and to which all parents were invited. Edward was particularly fond of assemblies that took place at night.

He liked to see grownups sitting at child-sized desks, and enjoyed watching them hunt along the bulletin boards for their own child's test papers or drawings, or whatever the teacher had hung there. They always pretended to be interested in the other children's work, too, but they really weren't and everyone knew it. He liked the assembly room itself, crowded and noisy and stuffy, with the parents talking and laughing and waiting, and the children peeking at them through the curtain, and Miss Hargraves, who was his and Rod's fifth-grade teacher, playing the piano.

The skit that they were doing for the assembly was called *Pandora and Her Box*. The class had been studying Greek myths, and Pandora, so it was told, had been the first woman. She had been made by Zeus, by hand, to be a trouble to Prometheus, who'd stolen fire from the gods. Pandora had been given a great beautiful box, which she was told never to open, but, being a nosy girl, she'd naturally opened it. And that, according to the Greeks, started all the misfortunes of mankind. Because out of Pandora's box flew the troubles and pests and sorrows that have bothered people ever since. Sickness and anger and evil and hatred and plagues and bad times and sadness, and every unpleasant thing that you could think of. They'd had a fine time in class thinking of one for everybody except Ruth Ann and Connie. Connie was Pandora. Ruth Ann, who was silly, but also pretty and blond, was to be the one good thing that flew from Pandora's beautiful, terrible box. Ruth Ann was Hope.

The mothers had made the costumes at home, and Ruth Ann's was all tinsel and tulle. She had a

46

gold crown to go on her head, and everyone had to agree that she looked very hopeful. Rod was Poor Sportsmanship. He wore a tattered baseball suit and a cardboard mask with a mouth that went down to his shoulders and India ink tears spilling on his cheeks. Edward was Anger. Mrs. Frost had made him a coverall in shades of red. His mask had tissue paper flames shooting from the eyes.

Oh, it was going to be a fine skit, all right. Edward didn't doubt it would be the best of all.

On the afternoon of assembly day, all the classes were to have a dress rehearsal. No schoolwork at all. Edward decided not to take his bike that morning because he had to carry his costume in a cardboard box. That, with his lunch, would make bicycling uncomfortable. It was a balmy, sunny morning, and he was walking along in good spirits till he heard the pound of familiar feet behind him. Not stopping to look, he ran, hoping to reach Rod's house before Martin could catch him. But, only half a block away, he was overtaken, and Martin, looking huge, planted himself in the way.

"*Good* morning, Weird One," he said. "What have you got in the box, huh?"

"Dynamite," said Edward with nervous anger. "You touch it and we'll both be blown up, Fatso."

47

"Oh, yeah?" said Martin nastily.

In the back of his mind Edward knew that if he didn't always answer this way, if, instead of running and then being . . . what was the word? . . . sarcastic . . . if, instead of doing those things, he stood still and said meek "Yes-Martin, anything-you-say-Martin" sort of things, he would not be tormented this way. But the back of his mind was one thing, and his feelings were another. Pursued by Martin, he ran, and faced by Martin he made these angry, stupid jokes, and, as far as he could see, the situation was getting worse all the time.

"You're a real funny little man, aren't you?" said Martin.

Edward gripped his box and said nothing.

"*Aren't you?*"

Silence from Edward. His arms, holding the box so tightly, were beginning to ache, but just the same Martin snatched it from him and threw it on the ground. Part of the costume burst out and trailed on the sidewalk. Martin put his foot on it, thrust his face into Edward's, and said, "Well, now, I just guess you'd better say uncle. Just for practice, like."

Edward drew a deep breath, bit his lip, saw, without looking down at it, his red costume under

Martin's great foot. "Uncle," he said, staring at Martin's chest. His lips felt stiff and his jaws ached. He waited.

After a moment Martin stepped back, laughed, and sauntered off to school. He was whistling. Edward stared after him for a long time, then bent and stuffed his costume back in the box and continued on his way to Rod's.

"Good morning, Edward," said Mrs. Graham, as he arrived. "What a lovely day, isn't it?" She looked more closely at him. "Why, what in the world is wrong, dear?" she said.

Edward shook his head and coughed. "Nothing, ma'am."

"But you look white."

Again Edward shook his head. "It wasn't nothing. Anything. Rod here?"

"He left for school a little while ago. I guess he thought you weren't coming this morning."

"I got held up," said Edward. He started off, then turned and said, "Is the baby born yet?"

"Maybe today," said Mrs. Graham with a big smile.

"That's good," said Edward.

At school, everyone was bustling around the classroom talking and yelling and laughing. Edward marched to his desk, shook his costume out and studied the dirty part where Martin's foot had been. Rod came over and looked too.

"What happened?" said Rod. "You drop it?"

"It got dropped for me," Edward said grimly.

"That Hastings again?" said Rod. Edward nodded. "You know," Rod said, "Martin Hastings oughta fly out of that Pandora's box. He'd be the biggest pest of all."

"And he wouldn't even need a mask," Edward said.

They were laughing when Miss Hargraves came over and said, "Got your costumes, boys? Oh my, yes. This *is* an angry-looking affair, Edward. Your mother did a wonderful job."

"It got stepped on, Miss Hargraves. See how dirty it is here? I don't know how to get it out."

Miss Hargraves picked up the red coverall and examined it. "I think some dirt on it is a good idea," she said. "After all, you wouldn't expect Anger to look as if he'd just come out of the laundry, would you?"

Edward looked at Miss Hargraves with respect. "I guess some dirt is okay," he said.

"Maybe I'll step on mine," Rod said thoughtfully.

"Well, don't overdo it." Miss Hargraves smiled and moved on to where Ruth Ann was mincing in her tinsel and tulle. "Ruth Ann," she said, "you aren't Tinker Bell. You're Man's Hope. You must move gracefully, with dignity. . . ."

Edward, pulling on his costume, forgot about Martin.

That evening, after dinner, Mr. Frost drove Edward to school and then returned home to wait a while with his wife. The parents were not to arrive until half an hour after the children, so that there would be time for getting into costumes and setting up props. Since the fifth grade was the next to last with its skit, they merely had to sit over at one side of the assembly room, in their regular clothes, and wait. This was difficult and they got noisy, and once Miss Hargraves said she was going to call the whole thing off. Of course they knew she wouldn't, but they did quiet down, because after all she couldn't play the piano and boss them too. They were pretty good at behaving when there was no one there to make them.

And, at last, the parents arrived, with a lot of looking and waving and talking to each other and the anthem was sung, and the curtain went up, sort of crookedly, and the kindergarten children were on the stage being a garden of crepe-paper flowers waking up in the spring. On and on went the presentations. Edward twisted in his seat to find his parents and wave to them. Mr. Graham was sitting with them, but not Mrs. Graham.

"Where's your mother?" he whispered to Rod.

"At the hospital. I guess the baby's getting born tonight. At last."

So now Rod would be an uncle again. Edward sat and thought about this. It was funny that *uncle* could be such an awful word when you were being made to say it, and yet being an uncle, like Rod, or having an uncle, like his own traveling Uncle Josh, could be so nice. And yet, when people were having a friendly wrestle, "say uncle," wasn't such an awful term. He decided that it all got back to Martin Hastings, who could probably make "lemon meringue pie" sound like poison.

Staring around the room, he noticed Mrs. Hastings. She wasn't looking at the stage, but at the ceiling, and every once in a while she yawned. Mr. Hastings wasn't there. Mr. Hastings never came to school things. Edward had once heard him say that he didn't have to go out of his *way* to be bored. With a sense of contentment, Edward looked at his own parents, who were applauding the end of the third-grade skit. *They* were not bored.

When the fourth grade came on stage, Miss Hargraves signaled from the piano with a nod of her head that her class was to make its way quietly around the side and up to the wings of the stage, where they would get into their costumes, except Ruth Ann and Connie, who'd been in theirs all along and so had had to stay behind the scenes while the rest of them sat in front. Connie was wearing what Miss Hargraves said was a simple flowing costume, very Greek. To Edward it looked like a sheet, but he supposed a sheet could flow. She also had a gold ribbon going across her forehead. Miss Hargraves called that a fillet. Rod and Edward thought it looked ridiculous, but the girls all liked it. Crums, thought Edward, looking at Ruth Ann and Connie, giggling as always, I'm glad I'm not a girl. He hoped that Rod's nephew, being born tonight, wouldn't turn out to be a niece.

As quietly as they could—which was pretty noisily—the fifth grade made itself ready. When the fourth had received its applause and gone to sit in the assembly room, the curtain fell, and the boys dragged the tremendous cardboard box they'd made in class to the center of the stage. It had been painted with pictures from a Greek fresco they'd had in their book, and inside were three small stepladders for them to climb up and leap from, shrieking, when Pandora threw back the lid. There was a door at the side through which they filed, Ruth Ann imploring people not to crumple her, and everybody else sort of jostling and enjoying it. Then Pandora, outside, tapped on the box, which was the signal for those inside to be quiet until the great moment when they could swarm yowling into ghastly view.

Outside, Pandora began in a high voice, "Oh dear, here is this box dear Father Zeus gave me but told me I must never never open . . ."

"Quit *pushing*," Ruth Ann whispered to somebody, while the rest of them milled and tittered in the darkness. And then Connie climbed the stepladder (garlanded) on the outside of the box and the lid flew back, and crash, bang, YOWL! they tumbled up the stepladders, out onto the stage, the afflictions of mankind in a tremendous tangle. After they'd stamped and cavorted and terrorized Pandora for a few minutes, Ruth Ann, all tinsel and tulle and gold tiara, climbed to the top of the box, waved her wand, and squealed, "I'm Hope! I am the Hope of Mankind!" She waved here and there to different parts of the audience, and smiled and bowed. Edward and Rod went into gales of laughter.

"Like she was running for president, or something," Rod gasped, and he and Edward rolled on the floor, which, as devils, they were supposed to do anyway. Ruth Ann looked at them scornfully, and repeated her message of comfort to the world.

On their way home, Mr. Frost said, "That was great, Edward, really great. Had me scared out of my wits until Hope showed up with her wand."

"That was Ruth Ann," said Edward. "You know that."

"Tonight she was Hope. And a very effective one, too."

"You were all effective," said Mrs. Frost. "I must say, I was *most* impressed."

Edward smiled with drowsy satisfaction. It had gone off splendidly. And what was even better, in the sixth-grade skit, Martin Hastings, who was supposed to blow reveille on his bugle, had boobled it something fierce. He'd had to try three times before he got it at all, and even then he'd sounded like a crow with indigestion.

Edward was thinking about this when his mother said, "I felt so sorry for Martin. But he *was* a good sport."

Edward sat up indignantly, all sleepiness gone from him. "Good *sport*? Martin Hastings? He couldn't be a good sport if there wasn't anything else left in the world to be. I practically laughed out loud at what a mess he made of a little thing like blowing that bugle he's been practicing on for eighty years."

There was silence, and then Mr. Frost said, "Well, I know someone who isn't being a good sport. That much is clear."

Edward thought he had never been so angry in his life. How much trouble had Martin Hastings caused him? How many caps had been snatched away and thrown in trees, how many times had his bike been knocked down, had *he* been knocked down? How many times had he been called Weird One in front of other people? And how many times did he complain to his parents? Practically never, that was how many times. And now his father said *he* wasn't a good sport? He looked at his father's profile and almost hated him.

"Edward," Mr. Frost said, in his explaining voice that Edward usually listened to but tried not to hear just now, "I'm not discounting the bully in Martin. And I'm not forgetting what a source of real trouble he is to you. Your mother said he was a good sport tonight, and he was. It took stamina to go on trying when he was having such a hard time playing his bugle, and in front of a big audience. And if you think it over, I believe you'll admit it."

Edward said nothing.

"Suppose it had been someone else," Mr. Frost insisted, and Edward saw that this was very important to him. "Suppose any other child in the school had stood up there and gone on trying after two such loud flops. Wouldn't you have said that kid was a good sport?"

"Well . . . yes," Edward said reluctantly.

"But you aren't willing to admit it in Martin."

"He's my enemy," Edward said. "I hate him."

But he sighed, and tried to suppose what his father had asked him to. What if it had been Rod, or David Seif, or Mike Toomy? He had to admit that then he'd have been all tense with them, and relieved when they finally played the thing—even badly—and he'd have called them good sports.

"Okay," he said. "I suppose he was. He was a good sport tonight. But he's never been any other time, and what good does it do to go being a good sport about a bugle once in your life if you're a bully and a dope all the rest of the time?"

"I don't know what good it will do Martin," said

58

Mr. Frost. "Some, maybe. But I was looking for the good it would do you to admit a thing when you see it, even in . . . an enemy."

Nothing more was said about it, but Edward, when he was in bed that night, frowned into the dark and thought hard. It seemed to be true, what his father had said. It seemed that he did feel better for having admitted, in this Martin that he detested, something that was good.

So it was a shame, and even Mr. Frost later admitted it was a shame, that the very first thing Edward saw when he got up next morning was Martin in the back-yard tree, making for the yellow wren house.

Edward leaned out of his window and yelled, "Listen, Fatso, you get away from that birdhouse or I'll . . . I'll kill you."

Martin, a couple of branches below the birdhouse, looked around as if in great surprise. He rested his elbow against the trunk of the tree, his cheek on his palm. One leg was drawn up on the branch and the other dangled down. Edward had never seen such an insolent and maddening sight in his life before. "Is that a fact?" said Martin, drawling like a TV outlaw. "You terrify me. I mean, you actually do. I'm shaking all over."

Edward, beside himself with rage, broke one of his own strictest rules. He ran for his father. "Dad!" he yelled, racing down the hall to the bathroom, where his father stood at the mirror shaving. "Dad, come here!"

"What is it?" Mr. Frost said loudly, dropping his shaver. "What's the matter?"

"That Martin—he's up in the tree and he's going after my wren house and I'm going to *kill* him if you don't do something."

Mr. Frost looked at his electric shaver, tested it, shook his head angrily, and remarked that anyway it was a good thing he didn't use a straight razor, and followed Edward to his bedroom. Martin was still lounging against the tree trunk.

"Martin," Mr. Frost bellowed. "Stop being such a pest. Get out of that tree this instant."

For a moment, Edward thought Martin would defy even grown-up authority, but then he moved reluctantly. "I wasn't doing anything," he said sullenly.

"Well, don't do it in our yard. And leave that birdhouse alone, do you understand?"

Martin didn't answer this time, but he dropped to the ground and walked away with his swagger showing.

61

Mr. Frost turned frowning from the window. "That's a fine way for a man to start his Saturday morning. Screaming out the window at the neighborhood children."

"Well, I'm sorry," said Edward. "Only he'd have done something, pulled it down or something, if I didn't call you. I want some wrens living there. That's why I made the house."

"I think it would be nice, too. But that's not the real point. You just can't allow a child to wreck things wantonly, and of course you had to call me. But what I don't understand is what in the world you *do* to that boy that he keeps after you this way?"

"Dad," said Edward, "*I* don't do anything. I just want to stay out of his way, see, and let him stay out of mine. But it don't work that way."

"Doesn't," said Mr. Frost.

"It sure doesn't," Edward agreed.

"But why?"

"I don't know why. And he isn't this way just with me. Everybody in school hates him, and he's always picking on smaller kids, and he's too old to be in the sixth grade anyway—"

"Oh, come now," Mr. Frost interrupted. "Let's keep this fair. Plenty of children get a year or so behind in school, through illness, or moving around, or one thing and another. That's no disgrace, and it's nothing to comment on."

"Okay," said Edward. "Okay. Leave that part out, there's still plenty wrong with him, and nobody likes him. I just want you to see that it isn't just me he picks on, but it's just me who lives next door to him. Wouldn't you like to work on a sheep ranch in Australia?"

"I certainly would not," said Mr. Frost. "And running away is never the solution to a problem."

Edward had heard this often enough, but he couldn't help thinking that moving away would be a good *start* toward a solution. He looked out at the wren house, bobbing gently in the tree. "He's contaminated it. Now no wrens will ever move in."

"He didn't even get close to it," Mr. Frost pointed out. He pushed Edward's clothes out of the way and sat down in the chair. "Sit over there, son." He gestured toward the bed. "We'd better talk this over."

"Ed! Edward!" Mrs. Frost called from downstairs. "Breakfast."

Mr. Frost got up and went to the door. "Edward and I are having a little talk, dear. We'll be down in a bit." He returned to the chair and sat rubbing his chin. Edward didn't think a talk was going to do much good, but still he felt a bit hopeful. So he looked at his father, and his father rubbed his chin, and there was silence, and presently Edward began to smile.

"What's the joke?" said Mr. Frost.

"You rub your chin like it was Aladdin's lamp. Maybe a genie's going to come out and give us the answer."

Mr. Frost gave a short laugh. "I guess I'm sort of baffled. You see, Edward . . . the essential thing with a bully is, he's unhappy."

Edward snorted.

"That's how I thought you'd react," said his father. "Nevertheless, it's true. A child bully—there are grown-up ones, too, unfortunately—but the child bully picks on people smaller than himself because the adults in his world have failed him. Grownups make him unhappy, but he *can't* pick on them, so his solution is to bully where he can get away with it."

"Yeah," said Edward thoughtfully. "That makes sense. So that's Martin's solution. What I want to know is, what's *my* solution?"

"Understanding, maybe?" To both of them the suggestion sounded a bit uncertain.

"You mean I'm supposed to understand that Martin's parents aren't awfully nice to him? So I understand it. So it still leaves him twenty pounds heavier than me."

Mr. Frost scowled and nodded. "He is pretty big."

"You said I should stand up to him. How can I stand up to him? He's bigger than you are!"

"Don't exaggerate." There was another long pause, and then Mr. Frost said, "I guess I was wrong about that. The standing up to him, I mean. Unless we taught you jujitsu."

"Hey," said Edward brightly. "How about that?"

"Now, Edward. You know I was joking. We'll just have to face it. You're younger than he is, and you're smaller, and if I were in that position, I'd run, too. If I made you ashamed of running, it was wrong of me. But it seems to me there must be some other way to work this out. I can't help feeling that if you really understood, you wouldn't be afraid of him. You'd be sorry for him."

"It's pretty hard to feel sorry for somebody who every time you meet him you wind up chasing your hat and rubbing the dirt out of your clothes. And it's pretty hard to feel sorry for somebody who calls you Weird One all the time."

"He does? What's the reason for that?"

"Ah . . . I think because I like to read. I don't think Martin knows how to read at all."

"Edward," said Mr. Frost loudly, "I will not have that kind of remark. In justice to yourself, I demand that you carry on this discussion fairly."

Edward saw what his father meant. His father was great for fairness, and the fact was Edward admired him for it, even when it got in the way, as now. "All right, Dad," he said. "I'll try to be fair. But he *doesn't* read anything but comics, and that's fair because it's true, and he thinks anyone who reads books is nuts. I mean, I'm not a book *worm*, like Mike Toomy, but a couple of times in recess I was reading a book I wanted to finish, so I did, instead of playing ball, I mean. And so smarty-Marty thought he'd call me Weird One and that would make everyone else do it."

"Has it?"

Edward shook his head. "Nope. Nobody but Martin. But he's got so many mean names for kids that nobody pays any attention. I told you, people don't *like* him."

"Poor Martin. He really must be unhappy."

In a pig's eye, thought Edward, but kept it to himself.

"I don't like to hurry you," Mrs. Frost called upstairs, "but everything's getting cold. Couldn't you continue the discussion down here?"

Mr. Frost stood up, ran his fingers through his hair so it stood on end, and said, "Well, we don't seem to have gotten much of anywhere."

"We got Martin out of the tree," Edward said.

They walked downstairs in silence, silently took their places at the breakfast table.

"What's it all about?" said Mrs. Frost.

"Martin," said Mr. Frost morosely.

"Oh, heavens. Again?"

"Still, is more like it."

Mrs. Frost put their plates in front of them. "Eat up while it's hot. Do you suppose it would do *any* good if I went over and . . . oh well, tried to have a talk with Mrs. Hastings?"

"Ruth Ann's mother had a talk with her," Edward pointed out.

"You wouldn't call that a talk. It was more like a duel at dawn."

"Old Mr. Eckman across the street had a talk with her," Edward mused. "And Mrs. Perkins on the other side of them had a talk with her. They all wind up as mad at Mrs. Hastings as they are at Martin."

"She's difficult," said Mr. Frost.

"She either won't admit there's anything wrong

with Martin, or she doesn't care," said Mrs. Frost. "I guess practically everyone on Barkham Street has had a go at her."

"Maybe you could join the Navy, Dad," said Edward. "We could travel."

Mr. Frost slapped the palm of his hand on the table. "Enough," he said. "I have had enough. We eat, sleep, and breathe Martin Hastings. It's beginning to give me heartburn."

"I must say I'm pretty tired of it, too," said Mrs. Frost.

Edward said nothing. The talk with his father had been interesting, but not really helpful. His mother had offered to see Mrs. Hastings, but everyone knew that was no use. They were tired of the whole thing, and he didn't blame them.

Only they weren't looking forward to a week's vacation side by side with an enemy who was growing meaner all the time.

"My electric shaver's broken," grumbled Mr. Frost. "Not your fault, really," he said to Edward. "But I wish you'd think before you yell. I'd come just as fast if you spoke in a normal voice, and there wouldn't be so many things getting broken."

"I'll try," said Edward.

All in all, Saturday was starting out to be a mess.

CHAPTER

5

Monday morning Edward sat on his front step, baseball cap on the back of his head, the sun warm on his bare arms. He was waiting for Rod, and while he waited was doing absolutely nothing. This was lazy and agreeable, and the sense of virtue was upon him strongly because this morning he had not only made his bed but had *offered* to run an errand.

He whistled softly and gazed along Barkham Street. All the trees were in full young leaf, rock gardens and flower borders brightened every house front. Through an open upstairs window he could hear his mother singing.

"The morning's at seven, the hillside's dew-pearled, God's in his heaven, all's right with the world," she sang, and Edward smiled. It was his mother's favorite song, and he was pretty fond of it himself. Softly, he whistled along with her.

Spring was in the air, God was in his heaven, and Martin was in Cedar Rapids with his parents. Everything was great.

Edward stretched, and waited for Rod, and grew lazy in the sunshine.

Two figures turned the corner of Barkham and Elm, a long way down the street. A man and a dog. Edward watched them idly as they ambled along, looking as if they didn't care if they ever got where they were going. Once or twice the man stopped to study a house number. Once he threw a stick for the dog, who hesitated and then decided not to bother. Edward fancied the man laughed, though they were still too far off to be sure.

On they came, easygoing, friendly, peaceful, and Edward watched them because he had nothing else to do, because they were strangers, because he always watched dogs. This was a collie type, and, as they grew nearer, Edward could tell that it was a young dog. Its white and brown fur shone and it moved on light little feet. The man wasn't young. He wasn't old, either. He had gray-brown hair, a tanned, lined face, he was slight, and he moved as lightly as his dog did. He wore khaki pants, a very white shirt open at the neck, a brown button-down sweater. He had a blanket roll on his back.

On they came, and Edward began to feel a peculiar soft thudding in his chest. He sat up straighter and waited, wordlessly. Could this be Uncle Josh? At last? This slight, light-moving man? He realized that until this moment he'd thought Uncle Josh would be a big, burly fellow in patched clothes, perhaps even with a bandanna-wrapped bundle slung over his shoulder on a stick. Like a hobo in a comic strip? Somehow the very thought seemed now unworthy.

On they came, and unconsciously Edward pulled the cap from his head and stood.

The man and the dog saw him, and then they too stood, a few yards away on the sidewalk, and they all looked at one another.

"Well," said the man, in one of the softest voices Edward had ever heard. "We meet at last, Edward."

"You're Uncle Josh."

The man nodded and moved forward, the young dog keeping at his side, and put out his hand which Edward took without being able to think of a thing to say.

The man released his hand and smiled and gestured toward the dog. "This is Argess," he said. "She probably could use a drink."

"Is she yours?"

"I don't really know. Let's say she's been traveling with me."

"She's young, isn't she?"

"Oh, yes. How did you know?"

"I know about dogs."

"Where's yours?"

"I don't have one."

"Oh?" The man said nothing more, but somehow Edward felt sided with. He tried to decide whether to tell about all the years he'd longed, in vain, for a dog, which would make Uncle Josh side with him more than ever, or whether in fairness to his parents he ought to point out about his lack of responsibility.

He hadn't made up his mind when the door behind him was flung open and his mother flew down the steps into her brother's arms. "Josh, Josh," she said, over and over, and a few tears fell down her cheeks. "Oh, here you are . . . my dear, dear Josh."

Argess wagged her tail and moved closer to Uncle Josh, but she kept her eyes on Edward, who was beginning to realize, with dawning rapture, that if Uncle Josh was going to stay here for a visit, so, of course, was his dog.

"I think I'll give Argess a drink," he said loudly.

Mrs. Frost, for the first time, noticed the collie at her brother's side. She looked down at Argess for a long time, then at her brother. "I might have known. Animals. Well," she sighed, "I suppose I should be glad it isn't a horse."

"Or a buffalo," said Uncle Josh. "I was out on the Great Plains for a while. Herds of buffalo there, Edward. But they've never been considered good pets."

Edward grinned. He leaned down, and for the first time put his hand on Argess' head. She seemed to dance a little, and her long pink tongue lolled gracefully to one side. "Can I take her in the house, to the kitchen, Mom?" he asked.

"May," said Mrs. Frost automatically. "May I. Yes, I suppose you may. Or must. I don't suppose there's anything I can do about it."

"Oh, now," her brother protested, "Argess is a charming dog. Neat and clever and full of heart."

"I'm sure she's all that," Mrs. Frost said. "It's just that . . . Oh, well. Give her a drink, Edward. And make her feel at home," she added dryly. She turned back to her brother. "You *are* going to stay with us for a while, aren't you? You aren't going to disappear in a few days, the way you did last time?"

Edward hadn't known about that, but he listened tensely for the answer.

"Sure I'm going to stay," said Uncle Josh. "As long as you'll have me. Or anyway, for a while. I've missed all of you."

"We've missed you," said Mrs. Frost, and Edward called Argess and ran with her into the kitchen. The small rug in the hall slewed beneath their feet, and while Argess was drinking he went back and straightened it, hoping his mother would notice this act of carefulness. But she was still out in front, talking with her brother. It was as if they couldn't interrupt this meeting long enough even to come inside.

Edward returned to the kitchen and squatted beside Argess, whose pink tongue eagerly scooped at the water, though she looked up briefly and her tail swung in greeting. Edward rested a hand on the rough fur of her back and just left it there. They were in this position when Rod appeared at the kitchen door and stood, wide-eyed, watching them.

"A dog," he whispered. "You got a dog, Edward."

Edward took a deep, blissful, wistful breath, and shook his head. "Not mine. She belongs to

75

my uncle out there. My Uncle Josh. Did you see him?"

"I met him," Rod said indifferently. He approached Argess. "He's a she?" Edward nodded. "Like my nephew," Rod said. Edward nodded again. Rod's nephew had turned out to be a niece, a great disappointment to Rod, though the rest of his family had seemed to take it pretty well. Rod wasn't feeling altogether happy about either his niece or his nephew these days, because it appeared they were all going to move into his house. His sister's husband was being sent to a foreign office for six months, and his sister had decided her children were too young to travel. Rod had done a lot of complaining about this over the weekend, but, at the sight of Argess, neither boy could think of anything else.

They sat beside her on the kitchen floor, Rod accidentally knocking over what was left of the dish of water. Edward wiped the spill with a dishcloth, and then thought his mother probably wouldn't approve of that, so he got up and rinsed it, and sat down again.

"What's her name?" said Rod, leaning forward to look in the dog's face. She licked his nose and he smiled with rapture.

"Argess."

"How do you spell it?"

"I don't know."

"She's beautiful."

"She sure is," said Edward.

"How long's she going to be with you?"

"As long as my Uncle Josh is."

"How long's that?"

"He said quite a while."

"Crums," said Rod, and grew silent.

But though the boys were content to sit, each with a hand in her thick fur, and look at her, Argess soon grew restless. She got up and started for the hall, whimpering a little, her nails pattering on the linoleum.

"Looking for my uncle, probably," Edward decided. "She's a loyal type dog."

"Not a one-man dog," Rod said. "One-man dogs are vicious. A collie is never a vicious dog."

"Oh, no," said Edward. "After she gets to know me, she'll like me. And you, too," he added kindly. "You're around so much she'll get to know you, too."

"I'll probably be around plenty, from now on," said Rod. Edward wasn't sure whether this was altogether because of Argess, or partly because of

77

the people who were going to be filling up Rod's house.

Argess by now was in the living room, where Mrs. Frost and her brother were sitting. She trotted to the man, lay down beside him in a composed, possessive way, and was still. The boys stood in the doorway, Rod simply watching the dog with loving eyes, Edward waiting to see what his mother would say to an animal in the living room. What she would say, in fact, to the whole idea of an animal in her house. He didn't see how she could ask Argess to leave without asking her brother to leave, too. On the other hand, the dog question was very big in his family, and so was his mother's insistence that there was not to be one until Edward got more responsible.

He felt in his heart and in his bones responsibility rising by the minute, but how to make his mother recognize it? He began to wish he hadn't announced, over and over in the past, that the sense of duty was now so strong in him that there really wasn't room for anything else. No one believed him, and he had to admit there wasn't much reason why they should. "Your sense of duty," his father had said, "usually lifts its shy head when you want something, and then disappears immediately, whether you get what you want or you don't. Not very reliable, now is it?"

Edward felt a lot of sympathy for that boy in the fable who'd cried, "Wolf, wolf. . . ."

Everyone but Uncle Josh was looking at the dog. He was looking fondly around the room, as a man will who returns to a loved place after a long absence.

"She's a very quiet dog, isn't she?" Mrs. Frost said at last.

"Eh? Oh, Argess," said Uncle Josh. "Yes. She has dignity. Odd, in such a young dog. Does it bother you? That I have her, I mean?"

"The dog doesn't bother me," Mrs. Frost said slowly. She glanced at the two boys, who sidled into the room and sat down, as if in class. "I like dogs. What bothers me is that we—Edward and his father and I—have discussed this matter for . . . oh, for years. And Edward knows that he is not to have a dog yet. He isn't old enough."

"I had a dog when I was six," said Uncle Josh.

Edward and Rod glanced at each other.

"You had the dog, and Mother took care of it," Mrs. Frost said tartly. "I don't want to take care of Edward's dog. I want him to. It has something to do with character."

79

"Oh well, character," said Uncle Josh with a smile. "I wouldn't know anything about that."

Mrs. Frost just looked at him, not speaking.

"Still," Uncle Josh went on, sounding a little uncomfortable, "Argess here is not Edward's dog. I suppose she's mine."

"Suppose?"

"Let's say we met up and we're traveling together. I don't like to *own* anything, you know that. Especially something living. I don't even like the word 'own.'"

"I know," said Mrs. Frost, and added, "But you will take care of her?"

"Oh, now—" said Uncle Josh. He put a hand down and gently massaged the collie's head. "I'll feed her, if that's what you mean. Have up till now. No reason why I should stop."

"But, Josh, a dog in a suburban house requires more taking care of than merely feeding. For one thing, they have to be walked."

"Walked! I don't have to help Argess *walk*."

"Dogs aren't permitted to run loose in this town."

Uncle Josh looked horrified, and then indignant. "I never heard of such a thing. What sort of community have you got yourself into? Won't let dogs run. Why I—"

"There are very good reasons for it," said Mrs. Frost. She sounded exactly as if she were explaining a rule to Edward. "They destroy people's gardens, they frighten small children, sometimes they bite. And we live in a very *nice* community, Josh, which Ed and I happen to like and want to live in. Peacefully. Without violating rules. Argess can't run loose. You do understand, don't you?"

"All right, all right," said Uncle Josh, his brows drawn down. "*Walked,*" he repeated in a low voice. "Never heard of such a thing."

Edward, unable to keep still another second, burst out, "Mom, lookit, I got a great idea. Let *me* take care of Argess. I mean, walk her and feed her, and you know—take *care* of her. I can practice on her. And then you'll see if I've got some responsibility, huh?"

"I'll help," said Rod. "I'll get up every morning at five o'clock and come over here and help walk her, and my mother can see, too. I mean, about *my* responsibility."

"I never heard so much about responsibility in my whole life before," said Uncle Josh.

"I didn't think you'd heard about it at all," said Mrs. Frost. She looked at the boys, at her brother, and flushed a little. "I'm sorry. I shouldn't have said that."

"Perfectly all right with me," said Uncle Josh.

But Rod and Edward, defensive for this wonderful man, were reproachfully silent.

Mrs. Frost sighed and got to her feet. "I have to leave. I hate to, on your first morning, Josh, but this is my morning at the Visiting Nurse Association. I can hardly back out at the last minute."

"Of *course* not," said Uncle Josh warmly. "More of your volunteer stuff?"

"Yes," said Mrs. Frost. She stood uncertainly for a moment, and then smiled at her brother. "You'll find the guest room ready." She paused, changed it to, "Your room. It's good to have you here. Argess, too. She seems to be a lovely animal. Oh, and Rod—please don't get here at five in the morning. You're welcome to help Edward practice on the dog, but not at that hour."

"Okay," said Rod. "What time shall I?"

"Work it out among you. The three of you."

"I resign in favor of the boys," said Uncle Josh. "If they're going to practice responsibility, they won't want me interfering."

Mrs. Frost opened her mouth, closed it again, then gave that half-laugh of hers, and turned to Edward. "Don't forget the errand."

"What errand?"

"If you recall, dear, you offered to ride over to

Mrs. Ferris' for me and get those swatches of material. For the slipcovers I'm going to make."

"Oh, yeah. I forgot."

"Well . . . remember."

"Sure thing," said Edward, wishing she'd go, so he and Rod could talk to Uncle Josh and play with Argess. She did, after a few more words with her brother, and when she'd driven off, the two boys turned to the man, their faces alight, and waited for him to say something, anything.

What he said was, "What's all this stuff about responsibility?"

Puzzled, Edward tried to think of an answer, since Rod was clearly leaving it up to him. "I guess," he said at length, "that it's about how Rod and I don't have any. I mean, we *are* sort of careless. Leave stuff around, forget things, lose things. You know. Once I almost burned the house down."

"How?"

"Making cocoa. I forgot to turn off the gas and went away and a potholder caught fire, and then a roll of towels, and then the cabinets were starting, only Mom got here in time."

"When your mother and I were children, I once burned the roof off our house. She ever tell you about that?"

Edward shook his head. "How did you do it?"

"Oh . . . it was pretty simple. Sort of simple-minded, too, I'll have to admit. I put a magnifying glass in the rain gutter. It was full of dry leaves, and it hadn't rained for weeks, so there wasn't a bit of moisture anywhere. The sun burned right through that glass and set the leaves on fire, which was what I was trying to see if it *would* do, and it did all right. Only I'd forgotten it was there and had gone off somewhere or other. Like you. Burned the whole darned roof. Funny thing, it was your mother came home that time, too, and caught it and called the fire department before the whole place went. You sure she never told you about it?"

Privately, Edward thought that this was the last sort of thing his mother would be apt to tell him. She'd be too afraid he'd try it himself. She'd be wrong, of course. Probably.

He realized that his Uncle Josh took it for granted that he was talked about in the family. He'd be awfully hurt if he knew that he was practically never mentioned at all. Edward felt resentful toward his parents for this.

"No," he said. "She never mentioned that."

"What sort of things does she tell you about me?"

84

"Oh . . . just things. You know. Like . . . well, she says I'm an awful lot like you."

"Does she?" said Uncle Josh, sounding pleased. "I'm flattered."

"So'm I," said Edward proudly. He was getting fonder of his uncle every second, and madder at his parents.

"Say . . . uh . . . Mr. . . ." Rod, who'd been pet-

ting Argess all this time, looked up at Edward's uncle inquiringly.

"Name's Bowdoin. But you might as well call me Uncle Josh, same as Edward here. Mister doesn't sit too comfortably in my ear."

"Okay, Uncle Josh," Rod said happily. "Thanks."

"Rod's an uncle, too," Edward said.

"Are you now," said Uncle Josh. "You made it early."

"Yup," said Rod. "I've got a nephew and a niece."

"That must make you proud."

"Yes," said Rod doubtfully. "Sometimes, anyway. But they're all moving *in* with me. The whole shebang, except my sister's husband. He's going to Saudi Arabia."

"Arabia, eh?" said Uncle Josh dreamily.

"So there they're all going to be, everybody on top of everybody."

"Sounds like a handy houseful."

"Handy," said Rod in a bitter voice. "You know what? I gotta give up my room. It's going to be the nursery."

"What are *you* going to do?" Edward asked in outrage.

"Sewing room. They're gonna shove my bed in the sewing room. If you ask me, they'll have to stand it against the wall."

"Be quite a trick, sleeping that way," said Uncle Josh.

"That's what I said," Rod told him, grinning a little. "I said what were they going to do, tie me to bed at night?"

"What did they say?" Edward asked.

"Said it would fit. In a pig's eye, it'll fit. Or maybe just. I'll have to jump from the hall into bed. And what about my desk? That won't go in at all. Dad says it's only for six months. Where'd they get that *only* is what I want to know."

"Oh, it can seem a long time," Uncle Josh agreed.

The two boys looked at each other, then at the man who was fiddling with Argess' ears and gazing off into space. "Arabia," he murmured. "What do you know."

The boys didn't have to speak to each other to know that they were in agreement. This was the most wonderful human being they had ever met. He talked to them the way they wanted to be talked to. Humorously, easily, as if everything they said was justified and everyone was equal.

He didn't ask how old they were or whether they liked school. He thought it was outrageous that dogs should be chained, called responsibility "all this stuff," surrendered Argess to their care without a word. He went where he wanted to go, said what he wanted to say, and apparently didn't really do anything for a living.

Sitting beside Argess, they looked at Edward's uncle and hoped that they'd grow up to be exactly like him.

CHAPTER
6

They were in the back yard, Uncle Josh lying back in a canvas sling chair, his eyes half-closed. He'd taken off the brown button-down sweater and rolled up his sleeves. He was very brown, and the muscles in his arms stood out strongly, though he was thin.

Edward and Rod, racing around the yard with Argess, now tireless in the matter of chasing sticks, looked at the man from time to time and found him very interesting and strange. If they spoke to him, or approached him, he opened his eyes immediately, and smiled, and spoke with warmth and interest, as if he really cared about everything they said and thought. But as soon as they moved off he stopped looking at them and seemed to go away somewhere.

They couldn't explain it, but felt, as they had never felt with an adult before, that they could do mischievous, forbidden, even perilous things right in front of him and he wouldn't lift his voice to rebuke or stop them. In a way it gave them a splendid, unchecked, adventurous feeling (though they could not, at the moment, think of any forbidden thing they wished to do), but in another way they didn't altogether care for it. They kept wandering back to him, to remind him of their presence.

"At least," he said once, "you have a good big yard here. Must be close to an acre, isn't it?"

"Almost," said Edward, wondering what he meant by at least.

He decided that one of the reasons Uncle Josh didn't ask many questions was that he read minds, because he said now, "I say at least, Edward, not in a derogatory sense. It's simply that I get so unused to houses and streets. Gives me a cooped feeling at first when I get back to them."

"Where are you usually?" Rod asked.

"Oh . . . on the road. Bumming around." He used the word as if it didn't bother him at all.

"Bumming around where?" Rod insisted. Edward was glad his mother wasn't present.

"Most recently in Arizona. The desert. The Grand Canyon."

"Does Argess always go with you?" Edward asked. He and Rod sat down on the grass and Argess flopped beside them, panting.

"Argess and I are pretty recent acquaintances. As a matter of fact, I met her at the bottom of the Grand Canyon."

"Where?" said Rod. "I mean, how?"

"You want to hear about it?" the man asked. Both boys nodded eagerly, and Uncle Josh leaned back, his brown hands clasped behind his head, looking into space in a way Edward had already come to recognize.

"Little less than a month ago," said Uncle Josh, and thought for a moment. "Yup. Just about. I was working in a hotel in the Grand Canyon National Park. You boys know about the Grand Canyon? What it is?"

Edward nodded and Rod shook his head. "Not exactly," said Rod.

"Well, it's a gorge. A colossus of a gorge, of the Colorado River. If you want the statistics, it's about 220 miles long, a good mile deep, and it ranges in width from about four miles to eighteen or so. It is a wonder of wonders. You boys ought to see it sometime."

"Crums, wouldn't I like to," breathed Rod, and

Edward began to wonder if some day, maybe even some day this summer, his uncle would take him on—on the road. I wouldn't be any trouble, he thought. I'm a good walker. Maybe, if I behave real good, *real* good, from now on—

"I was, as I say, working in this hotel, as sort of a handyman," Uncle Josh went on, and Edward forced himself back to the present. "But one day I looked around, and all the desert was in bloom. . . . Ah, you should be on the desert when it's blooming. The cactus flowers, in every color you'd ever imagine, and the smell of sagebrush, and the sky so vast and blue and cloudless, and then that canyon . . . like a reminder of Eternity." He exhaled a long silent breath. "Oh, the desert's beautiful," he said in a spellbound voice. He sat with his body relaxed, but his head up and tipped a bit, as though he listened to something far off. Then he looked at them again, and smiled, and said, "Well, there it was, the desert spring. And there was I, in a bunkhouse with people and walls all around me and a man, who was empowered as my boss to tell me such things, telling me to get a rake and smooth the driveway in front of the hotel. I didn't even answer him. I went into the bunkhouse, packed my gear in the blanket roll, and left."

"Just like that?" said Edward, marveling.

"Just like that. I haven't found a better way to do things."

Edward wondered what his father would say to that, and found he didn't care. Something about this uncle with his farseeing eyes, his memories of vast, far places, his indifference to time or what was expected of him, made life here on Barkham Street dwindle somehow. The things that had seemed exciting, like the school skit, or the wren house, just seemed tame. And the things that had been frightening seemed foolish. What was Martin, anyway? A twelve-year-old hood, who'd be scared to death of anyone his own size.

Edward looked at his uncle, and listened to him, and inside him grew a passionate longing to take to the road with this man. The longing was so great that he couldn't even think how that would mean leaving his mother and father, his home, everything he knew. All that seemed so dim beside his uncle that he could hardly take it into account.

"Well," said Uncle Josh, "there's a trail with a beautiful name, Bright Angel Trail, that goes straight down the side of the canyon. It's steep, and it's narrow and a good deal longer than the mile drop, and lots of people hire donkeys to take them down. It's a sight. Bedizened tourists, perched on these little monk-gray donkeys, their eyes popping—the tourists', I mean—and their legs out stiff and half of them wishing out loud they'd never gotten *into* this—"

Rod and Edward laughed, seeing it all through the traveler's eyes.

"I waited till the donkey parties had gotten well on their way, and then started down on foot. Didn't have anything particular in mind, except I'd never been down at the bottom of the gorge. I'd stop every once in a while and look up and see maybe an old buzzard soaring around on his spiky wings in all that blue sky. And way, way down below there was the Colorado River, winding along like a great boa constrictor on its way to lunch. And the red walls of the canyon dropped straight down so it made you dizzy to look. Took me hours to get to the bottom. And then, just about at the bottom, I met this heavy-set fellow coming up, and he had about the maddest, meanest expression I've seen on a human being. And behind him was this pup. She kept trying to get up and follow him, but she couldn't do it. She'd flop down, panting and gasping, and then she'd lift her head and whimper, and every time she'd whimper, this big fellow would look around and mutter and then face forward and keep climbing."

"He was gonna *leave* her," Edward said unbelievingly.

"He was. I said to him, 'Is that your dog?' and he said, 'If it's any of *your* business, she *was* my dog, but I don't intend to take her on as luggage. I didn't ask her to follow me down. She can follow me up or stay there, but I'm not carrying her.' And he kept on climbing. I was going to shout after him, but, as I say, he was kind of a big fellow with an ugly expression. I figured he'd just as soon poke me as look at me, and I don't have the build or the disposition for being poked by big ugly fellows."

"What would you do if he did?" Edward interrupted, really wanting to know.

Uncle Josh took a little time to answer. "Well, I'll tell you, Edward," he said at length, "I suppose I'd have to try to poke him back. Intellectually, I see nothing wrong with running when you're obviously outweighed, but men don't always react intellectually—"

"I do," Edward said shortly, and his uncle looked astonished. "I mean, I suppose I do, because I always run."

"When?" said Uncle Josh.

"When this guy—he lives next door, only he's in Cedar Rapids with his folks this week—goes for me. You'll meet him. I mean, see him. He'll be back in time for school, unless he gets run over or something."

"Bloodthirsty, aren't you?"

"No, he isn't," Rod said. "You just never saw Martin. He's mean. *And* big."

"Why is he mean?"

Both boys shrugged. "Search me," Edward said. "Dad says because his parents don't give a hang about him. Dad says bullies pick on other kids—smaller kids—because they're mad at their parents, only they can't pick on them."

"Don't his parents give a hang about him?"

"Oh, I suppose they do. Only they don't show it much. You know, it means something to a guy if he's in a play or something, if his parents come to look. Mr. Hastings never does. Once in a while Martin's mother does, but she always yawns and she doesn't ever talk to anyone else. She doesn't ever talk to anyone around here either, except when people go and ask her to tell Martin to cut it out."

"Cut what out?"

"Everything he does, practically. I mean, like I said, he picks on kids. And he sasses big people. Mr. Eckman gets red every time he sees Martin, ever since Martin was shooting arrows and one went through Mr. Eckman's hat. The hat was on Mr. Eckman's head. He said he might have been killed, and I guess he might've. Only Mrs. Hastings said well he wasn't, was he, and Mr. Eckman said if he ever saw Martin with an arrow again he'd call the police."

"Yes?" said Uncle Josh, when Edward paused. "What happened then?"

"Oh, Mr. Hastings took Martin's bow and arrow away. Martin's always having things taken away, but it doesn't seem to do any good. Now he makes faces at Mr. Eckman and calls him old prune-face. I guess you can't call the cops for that, but Mr. Eckman gets awfully mad."

"And this Martin picks on you?"

Edward sighed. "Just about all the time. I live next door, see? But I got to admit, I run. If he catches me, he makes me say uncle. And I say it. It's that or get my face pushed in the ground. Sometimes both."

"It seems to be a real problem," said Uncle Josh. "And does he bother you, Rod?"

"Some. But I don't have as much trouble with him as Edward does. I expect because I don't see him so much. Besides, my mother says it takes imagination to be afraid. I don't have much imagination."

"Boy, I must have plenty," Edward said mournfully. He leaned over and stared into Argess' eyes. "Gee, her eyes are brown as they can be, aren't they? Like cocoa."

Rod, wriggling, said, "Uncle Josh—about that big fellow. On the trail. What *did* happen?"

"He went his way, and I went—the dog's. By that time she'd just given up altogether, and was lying there limp as an old piece of chamois. I felt her nose and sort of looked her over, and decided she wasn't sick, just plain exhausted."

"So what did you do?"

"Picked her up and carried her along to a grassy place near the river and we spent the night there." The boys were speechless with wonder, thinking what it would be like . . . all night by the river at the bottom of the great canyon. It seemed to them they'd never in their lives before met anyone who'd really lived.

"Can you see the stars from way down there?" Edward asked.

"Oh, sure. Bright and snapping and thick as a meadow of daisies. It was a fine night. The stars, and those black cliffs rising, and the sound of the river, and once in a while the bark of a coyote far away. And Argess, here, lying beside me, with her head on the blanket roll, snuffling in her dreams. . . ."

Uncle Josh stopped and looked far off to where the horizon would be if the houses on the next street hadn't blocked the view. To Edward, who'd always found his large back yard with its sweep of grass and its stand of trees more than adequate, everything seemed shrunken, hemmed in, dull. He looked at it through his uncle's eyes and was, if not ashamed, at least apologetic. He was considering how to let Uncle Josh know that he realized how cramped it all must appear, and at the same time not be disloyal to his parents, who were very proud of this house and acre. He hadn't come up with anything when Uncle Josh resumed talking.

"She was fine in the morning. Starving, of course, but fine. I opened a can of hash and we shared it, and then walked back up the trail before the donkey parties started. And . . . here she is.

Been walking with me, sharing the way, ever since."

"You walked all the way from Arizona to here?" Rod asked.

"We got rides pretty often. Surprising how many people will pick up a man with a dog. Especially a dog like Argess. She looks so reliable."

"Why did you call her Argess?"

Uncle Josh smiled. "That was a whimsy. You boys ever heard of Ulysses?"

"Sort of," said Edward. "He was in the Trojan War."

"That's right. Well, if you remember, Ulysses hardly hurried home when the war was over. He wandered. Well, I'm a wanderer, too. And I remembered that Ulysses had a dog named Argus, so it seemed fitting for me to name this one Argus. But his dog was male, and our friend here is a female. So, I called her Argess. A-r-g-e-s-s. Ess is a feminine suffix. Do you know what a suffix is?"

Ron wrinkled his nose. "During vacation I'd rather not."

Uncle Josh laughed. "Well, that's the story."

"How does it end?" said Edward. "I mean, is she going to go on wandering with you, or—" He scarcely dared finish, and he felt Rod's eyes on him, full of hope.

Uncle Josh, however, didn't seem to get the point. He stretched and yawned and said who knew what the future held, personally he never even wondered. Then he appeared to withdraw again, and presently the boys left to throw sticks for Argess. They played with her all day, and when in the late afternoon Rod had to go home, they asked Uncle Josh whether they could tie a rope around her neck so that Edward (who certainly wouldn't leave Argess behind) could accompany his friend.

"A rope?" said Uncle Josh, frowning. "Why a rope?"

"You know," Edward explained. "On account of not letting her run loose."

"She isn't running loose if she's right beside you, is she?"

"But what if she doesn't stay?"

"She'll stay with you," said Uncle Josh. "She does what's expected of her, even when it's unreasonable, which I consider this ordinance to be. Highly."

Edward thought his mother, who was present at this conversation, was going to complain. But she didn't. She stared fixedly at her brother for a moment, said, "Be back fairly soon, dear," to Edward, and went toward the house. "I'll have to be starting dinner," she called over her shoulder.

Rod and Edward mounted their bikes and started off, calling Argess, who hesitated and glanced at Uncle Josh.

"Go along with them," he said, and she shot after the bicycles.

Once, on the ride over, she cut off Edward, who nearly fell but steadied himself in time.

"She isn't used to bikes," he said.

"Or boys," Rod added. "But she likes us all right."

Edward agreed happily that she seemed to. She caught on quickly to the trick of running beside a bike without bumping it, and, as Uncle Josh had predicted, she stayed right with them.

"I think," said Rod, "that your uncle sort of gets your mother mad."

Edward thought so, too. "I guess because he doesn't pay much attention to rules," he said. "My mother believes in rules."

Since the boys had also been brought up to believe in rules, neither knew what to say. A man like Uncle Josh seemed above and beyond rules, somehow. At the same time, Rod and Edward felt that on the whole their parents were usually fair about things and often right. Even when the boys were angry, even when they argued and protested, as Edward did about baths, or Rod over giving up his room, they hardly ever felt they were really being treated unjustly, or told things that were not so. And their parents said that laws—and rules—were made for reasons and were to be observed.

Since it was too puzzling to work out, they stopped talking about it.

At the Graham house, Mrs. Graham was on the lawn, getting Rod's nephew out of his playpen. She looked up in surprise at the sight of Argess.

"Did your folks break down and get you a dog, Edward?" she asked, not sounding very pleased.

"No, ma'am. This is my Uncle Josh's dog. He's visiting. So is she. Her name is Argess."

"Well, don't let her get near the baby."

Rod scowled. "Mom, can't you see she's sitting down and not even trying to get near the baby?"

"Well, I was just saying."

"So was I," Rod muttered.

His mother gave him a keen look. "Are you still fretting about your room, Rod? I must say, you aren't being very co-operative. What would you expect your sister to do, camp out on the lawn with her babies?"

Rod brightened. "No. But I would. Hey, how about that, Mom? Could I? Edward could bring something to sleep in, and—"

"My uncle's banket roll, maybe," Edward said, catching Rod's fire. "Yeah, I bet he'd lend it to me, and we could cook out and everything. Or we could do it in my yard. It's bigger. Or—" He faltered, thinking of Martin.

Mrs. Graham laughed. "Honestly. You two." She turned toward the house, the baby struggling in her arms. "This young man wants his supper."

"You mean we can't?" Rod demanded. "What's the matter with that idea?"

"Now, Rod."

"No, but listen, Mom," said Rod, following her. "If you'd just listen for a minute. Why *can't* we? The weather's good. If I went on a hike, you wouldn't mind."

"A hike is one thing. Living like a gypsy in your own back yard is another. Anyway, you still have your room. Your sister and the baby won't be here for several days yet." She went in the house, closed the screen door behind her, saying, "Don't go away again, dear. Your father will be home in a few minutes. 'By, Edward." She looked at Argess sitting between the boys, her ears up, eyes alert, pink tongue lolling. "That *is* a nice dog," she said, and then went toward the kitchen with her now howling grandson.

Rod sat down on the lowest porch step and exhaled a long defeated breath. "I don't know," he said. "It's so hard to figure them out. Sometimes they're so reasonable, and sometimes . . . What the heck's *wrong* with sleeping out in the yard?"

"I don't know," Edward said. "I suppose she'd worry. I know my mother would. She'd be up and down all night, peeking to see if wolves had eaten me, or something."

"The only thing that could eat you in your own back yard is mosquitoes. Or Martin, I suppose, if we slept in yours."

"Not if we slept there this week." Edward pondered for a moment and then said, "Why don't we go in and ask her could you come up and just sleep out one night, in my yard? Maybe she doesn't want you *living* out there, like you said. I don't think you'd like it anyway. Suppose it rained?"

"I bet rain doesn't stop your uncle."

They considered Uncle Josh for a moment. Out

in all kinds of weather, with no one telling him what to do, or where to go.

"When did he start being a wanderer?" Rod asked.

"Ran away. When he was sixteen, I think my mother said."

"Crums."

Edward got up. "I suppose I better go home. You gonna ask your mother first about sleeping out?"

"Tonight?"

"Why not? It's nice weather."

"Okay. You wait here. I don't think maybe we better take Argess in the house." Rod shot through the door and was gone for several minutes. When he came out, he was grinning. "All set. My mother called your mother, and they don't either one of them like it, but they say okay, if we're careful. I didn't ask them careful of what. I'm gonna bring up a couple of blankets and Uncle Josh is gonna show me how to make a blanket roll. Wait a minute." He was gone again, and this time he took longer.

Edward lay on the grass with Argess. He'd discovered that whenever he lay down and closed his eyes, Argess would gently grasp his shirt in her teeth and try to pull him up. They played at this tirelessly until Rod returned.

He had some blankets and a package of hot dogs. "We'll make a cookout. Maybe we can get your Uncle Josh to come out and spend the night, too, huh?"

"Hey, yeah. I bet he'd like it."

But Uncle Josh, when they got back to Edward's and put the proposition to him, shook his head. "My dear young fellow, this is the first night in how many I can't recall that I've been able to look forward to a dinner involving linen and good silver, and a bed that has a roof over it. I'll be glad to help set you up, and supervise in any way you think I can. But share your adventure I will not."

The boys were more disappointed than they wanted to say. Still, they supposed he was being reasonable. Mrs. Frost contributed potato chips, carrots, and a thermos of cocoa and some cake to the cookout, but Edward knew she wasn't very happy about the idea. She looked at her brother once and said he'd certainly started something, and Uncle Josh said he didn't know what, all boys slept out occasionally and they could hardly have selected a tamer place to start. He caught Edward and Rod looking at him when he said that, and added immediately, "The basic idea is the same, boys. You're out, under the sky, on the ground. Sleeping out is sleeping out, no matter where it's done."

But of course they didn't believe that, and some of the fun seeped away, even as they made their preparations.

During this time, Argess was sitting on the back porch, and no real decision had been come to as to whether she would, while Uncle Josh remained, be allowed in the house. She'd only been in that once in the morning. Mrs. Frost had fed her on the back porch, and now she lay there, head on her paws, watching them through the screen door as they moved about the kitchen.

Suddenly she sat up, and a moment later Mr. Frost appeared at the kitchen door.

She hears people before we do, Edward thought. She'd be a good watchdog. "Hi, Dad," he said, and Rod said, "Hi, Mr. Frost."

Mr. Frost greeted them both and then turned with a broad grin to Uncle Josh. "Well, well, well," he said, putting out his hand. "You made it. By gosh, it's good to see you."

The two men shook hands heartily and then thumped each other on the back. Edward noticed how pale his father looked, in comparison to Uncle Josh. His face didn't have as many lines, and he was bigger, but Mr. Frost, in his business suit, with the loosened tie and the jacket hanging over his arm, looked tireder and somehow older than his brother-in-law. Edward had a sudden, unexpected feeling of protectiveness. He remembered how his father had talked a couple of weeks ago when they first knew Uncle Josh was coming. His father had sounded as if he'd like to wander, too. Maybe, thought Edward, all men do. Only, of course, all men couldn't. They had to work and take care of their families.

"Dad," he said affectionately, "we're gonna sleep out tonight, Rod and me. Would you like to, too?"

Rod, who was definitely off grownups for the moment, threw him a warning glance, but Edward ignored it. "We're gonna cook out, and every-thing."

Mr. Frost hesitated. "Well," he said, hanging his jacket over the back of a chair and putting his brief case on the floor, "it's tempting, Edward. But I guess I better not. I have a hard day coming up tomorrow, and I don't know how it is, but every time I sleep out the only rock within miles is under my back, and grizzly bears appear. Imported, I suppose."

"Ed," said Mrs. Frost reproachfully. "You'll frighten them."

The boys and the two men laughed, and, after a second, so did Mrs. Frost. "Nevertheless," she said, "I still am not completely happy about this."

"Then it's a good thing they didn't invite you," Uncle Josh said.

"*Say,*" said Mr. Frost, walking over to the door. "Say, what have we here?" He opened the door, and Argess, after a pause, walked in, waving her tail.

"That's Argess," said both boys.

"She's Uncle Josh's."

"She wanders with him and he found her at the bottom of the Grand Canyon."

Mr. Frost was petting the collie and smiling. "What a peach of a dog," he said, and Edward and Rod breathed deeply with pride. Edward glanced quickly at his mother, to see how she was taking the dog's presence in the kitchen. She was biting her lower lip and staring at Argess, who suddenly lifted her cocoa-brown eyes and stared back. The dog and the woman looked at each other for a long moment, and then Mrs. Frost said, "She is nice. So oddly well behaved." Nobody said anything. "I suppose . . . Well, if we left her out all the time, she'd have to be tied when someone wasn't with her."

"No, she wouldn't," Uncle Josh said. "If we tell her to stay close to the house, she'll stay."

"What Mom means," Edward said anxiously, "is she's trying to decide if Argess should be allowed in the house, Uncle Josh. Furniture and all," he pointed out vaguely, but they all understood what he meant.

"Well, if we can keep her out of the living room," Mrs. Frost said. "After all, I am making new covers—"

"Oh, sure," said Edward and Uncle Josh together.

"Then I suppose it'll be all right." And she said again, as if reassuring herself, "Her manners are excellent."

"Look here," said Mr. Frost. "I'm going up and take a quick shower, and then I'm coming down and I want to hear every darn thing you've done in the last ten years, Josh."

"Oh, it wasn't ten years ago I was here," said Uncle Josh. "More like six or seven, wasn't it?"

"Whatever," said Mr. Frost. "Seems like more

than ten. Excuse me, everybody." He started away, turned back and gave Argess a quick pat, and dashed off. They heard him take the steps two at a time, and then his whistle as he strode down the hall.

Edward thought, Dad's all excited about seeing Uncle Josh and hearing about the wanderings. It occurred to him again that maybe at heart his father was a wanderer, too. Only now it wasn't altogether a warm, nice thought. He was brooding on it a little, but his mother's next words drove it from his mind completely.

"Edward," she said, "where did you put the swatches?"

"Swatches?" said Edward, after a long pause. "Oh, yeah, the swatches. From Mrs. Ferris, you mean."

"Yes, dear. Where did you put them?"

Edward took a deep breath. "I . . . Well, it's like this, Mom—"

"You forgot them."

"Well, as a matter of fact . . ." He stopped, waited, and went on. "Yeah. I forgot them."

He stood there, feeling awful. After his mother had been so nice about Argess, about the cookout, now he had to go and let her know that he was

113

still as careless as ever. It wasn't very often that his own thoughtlessness bothered Edward. He left that to his teachers and parents. But it bothered him now. He couldn't even bring himself to make excuses.

Mrs. Frost made them for him. She said it had been an exciting day, and probably she'd have forgotten too, and tomorrow would do just as well. But Edward knew there'd been plenty of times today when he could have gotten those swatches. For the first time he was really annoyed with himself for forgetting something he'd said he'd do. For the first time, too, he didn't make a whole lot of promises to his mother about how he'd do better in the future.

He petted Argess, and tried to make a promise in his mind.

CHAPTER

7

He never noticed when the wrens came. One day the wren house swung emptily from its branch, almost forgotten by Edward, who'd worked so hard over it, and the next day, when he got home from school, his Uncle Josh called from the back yard and said, "Look up there, Edward. You have house guests."

Sure enough, there were two wrens, little and brown and busy. One was sitting on a twig, as though supervising, and the other was inside, trying to pull a straw through the tiny round door. He'd grasped the middle of the straw with his beak, and it stretched across the front of the house, refusing to bend. The wren refused to let it go. Edward and his uncle watched the struggle with interest. Finally, after a good deal of twittering from his mate, the bird backed into the house and the straw slowly bent, slowly was pulled inside.

In a moment the wren reappeared, and both small birds flew off. Searching, Edward decided, for more material.

"Well," said Uncle Josh, "they're going to be a long time getting settled in, if that's the way they're going to go at it."

"Gee," said Edward "I'm awfully glad they came."

"It's always a satisfaction to have some wild creature accept something you've offered it. Men have pretty well succeeded in getting all animals to hate them, and I suppose basically most of us are sorry. Which is why we get such a kick out of it if an elephant consents to eat our peanut, or a bird actually uses the house we build for him. We're always trying to get them to love us. When we aren't killing them for food. Or for fun. See, there they come back again."

This time the wrens had a little twig and a bit of string. One sat outside and waited while the other arranged his finding inside.

"But they don't love us, do they?" Edward said suddenly.

"Nope. They use us, and we should be grateful even for that. We've certainly used and misused them."

"Dogs love people."

"Oh, dogs are different. Cats, too, maybe. Though I'm not so sure about them. Something of the wild thing remains in a cat. Dignity. Self-sufficiency."

"Argess is dignified."

"Right you are. For a young dog, it's amazing. I sometimes think she must have associated with cats in her very early days. She has that proud, mysterious air. You know something, Edward, if we cut some short lengths of string and hung them on the lower branches of that tree, I'll bet your wrens would be glad to make use of them. Not now. We don't want to alarm them. But say tonight, after they've gone to bed."

"I never heard of that."

"Sure. They like things like that. My mother used to put the combings of her hair on a privet hedge for the birds. They were especially fond of it. She had long brown hair. Should think it would have been very nice for a nest."

"She was my mother's mother, too."

"Yes," said Uncle Josh.

"I never met either her or your father. My grandfather. I mean, that grandfather. Dad's mother and father come to visit us at Christmas. They're very nice."

"I'm sure they would be," said Uncle Josh. "So were your other grandparents," he added pensively. "Lovely people."

They were silent for a while, sitting with Argess

between them, watching the wrens work at house-building. Edward was pleased and proud at their presence, and he wondered if a pair had moved into Rod's birdhouse, too.

"Maybe I could get some of Mom's hair," he said, but Uncle Josh said probably hers would prove too short.

"My mother's hair was *long*. A bird likes to weave something like that in and out of the twigs and things. Makes the nest nice and soft for the eggs."

Edward turned his attention from the wrens and looked into his uncle's brown face. It was a very nice face, with its blue, dreaming eyes, its lines, its look of patience and humor. But it nearly always had that air of being not really with the person he was talking to, as if his mind was on something else, even when his eyes were on you. In some ways, Edward admired that, and yet it made him uneasy, too.

"Uncle Josh?" he said, a little too loudly.

"I'm right here."

"Yeah. Excuse me. Uncle Josh, why did you decide to run away from home? I mean, *how* did you?"

His uncle was silent so long that Edward began

to be afraid he'd offended. He was just about to apologize again when the man said, "I don't know that I can answer. I didn't really know then why I left, and I'm only slightly clearer about it now. I think because I can't stand *having* to do anything. I never could have stayed on a job, for instance, with someone *telling* me things. Oh, I take a job now and then, and put up with it, but that's because if I want to eat it's that or stealing. I don't want to be a thief. I take a job, and work long enough to lay a little by, and then quit. Usually without notice. It's very wrong of me, of course."

Edward thought so, too, but he didn't say so. Anyway, Uncle Josh was different from other people. Edward couldn't imagine his father quitting a job. Certainly not just walking off because it was spring. But his father and Uncle Josh, even though they got along so well, were very different from each other. Mr. Frost had always said that life was full of things you had to do, and responsible people simply did them. Edward supposed that Uncle Josh just wasn't a responsible person.

"Dad says your goal is Nature's heart, and—" he cast his mind back "—and the meaning of man."

A curious little smile moved over his uncle's face. "Is that what he said? Well, I'll tell you,

Edward, I think he's being too kind. I'm afraid my goal is avoiding goals."

"Do you think," Edward said tentatively, "that my father would . . . would like to be a wanderer, too?"

Uncle Josh considered. Then he shook his head. "Not really. Oh, all men get wanderlust from time to time. And boys do. Don't you, ever?" Edward nodded, but in truth he wasn't quite sure. He'd often thought he'd like to take a trip, but before now he'd thought of it as being with his parents. Lately, of course, he'd hoped to travel with Uncle Josh, but the fact was, he never had considered running away. He didn't quite want to say this to Uncle Josh. It sounded so unadventurous.

"But your father," Uncle Josh was going on, "is a man who loves his family, his home. He'd be miserable tramping around from place to place, without an aim, without ties."

Feeling considerably relieved, Edward ruffled the thick fur on Argess' neck.

"Uncle Josh, I got an idea."

"Let's have it."

"How about this . . . how about if after school is out, you and me and Argess take a trip together? I mean, just go on the road. Huh? How about it?"

"Now, wait a second, Edward. Give me a chance to think."

Wriggling with impatience, Edward gave him a chance. It took too long, and Edward was beginning to feel that whatever thinking his uncle was doing, it was not about this idea, when Uncle Josh began, very slowly, to speak.

"It's an idea," he said. "Only I can't figure if it's a good one or a poor one." He held up a warning hand, and Edward, who was about to interrupt, subsided. "I'd like it, mind you. In many ways. But I'm not at all sure your mother would. And I'm not sure you would."

"Oh, but—"

"You don't really have a notion what it's like, Edward. You think it's all sleeping under the stars and finding fine dogs . . . and speaking of sleeping under the stars—"

Edward scowled. He knew what that referred to. The night he and Rod had decided to sleep in the back yard. They'd lasted till what they thought was three or four in the morning (it turned out to be just short of midnight), and then had crept back in the house, itching hideously from mosquitoes, sore and cold from lying on the ground, and scared by something they never identified, though Mr. Frost was probably right when he said no doubt it was a dog running loose at night since he couldn't in the day.

"But that was different," Edward said now. "And besides, it was just us. Boys, I mean. I'd have *you*."

"You're very flattering," said Uncle Josh. "But what I'm trying to make you see is that being with me would be even worse. You'd have no house to go to when you got itchy and achey and scared."

"But I wouldn't be scared with you."

"You might. I'm not always exactly at ease myself. And if something went wrong . . . if you got sick . . . I don't know, Edward. You see, I've never traveled with anyone. Even Argess here was sort of a bother at times."

Edward's heart sank at the words. That was really what it came to. He'd be a bother to his uncle. "All the rest is just sort of an excuse, isn't it?" he said sadly. "What you don't want is somebody with you."

Suddenly his uncle leaned over and put his arm around Edward's shoulder. "I hope that isn't what I mean," he said. "It's just that I'm not a young man, and I've never had anyone with me. I think you'd make a fine traveling companion, Edward. I don't know if we can work it out, but, please believe me, you're the first person I've ever thought I could possibly travel with."

Caught between pride, pleasure, and an odd sort of pain at his uncle's words, Edward didn't know what to say. So he resorted to Argess' ears again, and then they watched the wrens for quite a while. Next door, Martin's bugle began to sound, and Uncle Josh winced a bit, but neither he nor Edward commented as the notes went on and on, sometimes clear and steady, sometimes falling to a shrill decline. After a while they got up and walked toward the front of the house where Edward often sat on the step at this hour, waiting for Mr. Frost to appear, trudging home from the bus stop.

"Oh, I'll be goldarned," said Edward, as they came around the driveway, "look at that, will you? He's gone and knocked my bike over again." He glanced over to where Martin's bike stood propped near the top of Mrs. Hastings' rock garden. "I'm going over and shove his down the bank."

"Now, wait a minute," said Uncle Josh. "Wait a minute. In the first place, how do you know Martin did it?"

"Because," Edward said patiently. "I just know.

Dopey Martin always tips my bike over if I forget and leave it up here. Mostly I put it in the garage, but if I forget, he shoves it when he rides by."

"Do you realize I only know Martin through his bugle? School's been open nearly two weeks and I've never laid eyes on him."

"He's got to come home and stay in and study every day. His father said so. Because he's not so hot at his schoolwork. I think it's great not to lay eyes on him. I guess you just haven't been around when he gets home and you oughta be glad. He's no treat to see."

"How do you know he has to stay in? Did he tell you?"

"Heck, no. I heard him telling another guy. I hope it goes on the rest of the year. I'm going over and knock down his bike."

"Wait a minute," Uncle Josh said again. "I think that's sort of stupid. He knocks yours down, you knock his down. It's so pointless."

"What am I supposed to do, just *let* him push it over?"

"You could remember to put yours in the garage."

"I could remember plenty of things," Edward

said. "Only I seem to forget better than I remember. Everything."

"You do, at that," said Uncle Josh absent-mindedly. "Look . . . go in the house and get me a sheet of paper and a crayon. A red one, if you can. And some Scotch tape."

"Okay. Why?"

"I thought we'd try a little strategy for a change."

"All right. But I think shoving's better."

When he came back with the paper and crayon, Uncle Josh thought for a moment, then laid the paper on the porch floor and wrote in big red letters: MY BIKE CAN LICK YOUR BIKE.

"There," he said. "Now, go over and stick this to his handlebars."

Edward grinned. "Well, it's funny. But I don't see what good it's going to do."

"It just seems to me that it might be possible to end this warfare, if somebody shows some interest in ending it. You don't want to keep this up forever, do you?"

"No. Only I still don't see the point."

The bugle in the next house slid into silence.

"If you two keep on playing tit for tat, shove for shove, with the same things being done over and over, there can't be any sort of break in the pattern between you, don't you see? This is a change. It might confuse Martin. It might even amuse him. Anyway, it's something different, and I think something different is what's called for."

Edward looked at his uncle fondly. What he thought was that Uncle Josh didn't know beans about Martin. But it was nice of him to be interested, and to try straightening things out. Anyway, it couldn't hurt. So he went over and fastened the note in the center of Martin's handlebars, and came back to his uncle. "Now what?"

"Now we wait until he comes out to put his bike away."

"Sometimes he doesn't put it away at all."

"Oh, well." Suddenly, in that abrupt way he had, Uncle Josh lost interest. He looked down the road, remarked that Ed was late, and said he thought he'd go in and read the paper.

"What about Martin?" Edward asked, but without much hope. Grownups—and Uncle Josh, different as he was in many ways, was no exception—grew bored with kid things. They'd stay with you up to a point, and then all of a sudden they'd want to hear the news, or take a nap, or do one of the many things that grownups did do. And, to tell the truth, Edward found *their* doings pretty boring most of the time. So it was all fair enough.

Philosophically, he settled down to wait for either his father or Martin to appear. He was betting with himself which would be first, and he lost, because Martin suddenly came out and started for his bike. Edward, secure on his porch, watched with interest while Martin stopped, surprised, then advanced and ripped the note from his handlebars. He apparently read it two or three times, and then he laughed, and glanced over toward the Frosts' house.

"Pretty funny," he said.

Edward felt a small stir of hope. He was a boy who was prepared to like practically everybody, and while he didn't think he could ever actually like Martin, it would be a relief not to have to hate him all the time. Maybe Uncle Josh had been right—

"I bet you never thought of it yourself, Weird One." Martin's lip curled a little.

Edward hesitated. "Not exactly," he said. "I mean, my uncle and I—"

"Oh, yeah," said Martin insolently. "Your uncle, I heard about him. The bum."

"He's a traveler," Edward said hotly.

"Bum is how I heard it."

And now the thing happened that Edward had always hoped would happen, but had never really expected to happen. Faced with Martin, and one of Martin's ugly remarks, he didn't stop to think, he acted. He ran, but this time it was straight for the enemy, and Martin was bowled over before he knew he was being attacked. Edward pounded into him with the strength of outrage, and, strong as Martin was, he took a punch in the eye and one on the head before he began to fight back. Edward felt himself being rolled to his back, but he kicked and punched and struggled, his breath coming in great gasps, his body wiry with hatred. He drove his fist into Martin's stomach as hard as he could, but it was his last punch. Martin grabbed his head and began to bounce it up and down on the lawn. In a confusion of pain, Edward thought that grass wasn't nearly as soft as it looked, and he supposed Martin was going to kill him.

Then into the fray came a cannonball of fur and teeth, and in spite of everything Edward's heart swelled with pride. Argess was defending him. She snarled and growled and thrust herself between them, scratching them both with her long nails, and finally getting a grip on Martin's shirt.

Martin let out a terrible howl, and then it seemed that everybody was there. Martin's mother, screaming and threatening. Edward's mother, pleading with Uncle Josh to make them stop. Uncle Josh, himself, pulling the boys apart and commanding Argess to let go. And dozens of neighbors all standing about in a curious circle.

Dirty, bloody, gasping, Edward and Martin were dragged apart. They stood in their ripped

clothing, glaring at each other, almost uncon-
scious of the lookers-on.

"What's going *on* here?" said Mrs. Frost. "Edward, what happened?"

"What happened," Mrs. Hastings said tensely,
"is that you have a vicious dog that attacked my
son and I'm going to call the police, that's what I'm
going to do—"

"The dog has nothing to do with it," Martin said,

astounding them all. His face was scratched and swollen, and he transferred his glare with reluctance from Edward to his mother. "It's this kid, this—"

"This child who's half your size," said Mrs. Frost, advancing so angrily that Martin backed up and Mrs. Hastings stepped forward, and for a minute Edward thought that two grown-up women were going to get in a fight, and go rolling across the lawn. Apparently Uncle Josh thought so, too. He burst out laughing, stopped abruptly when both women rounded on him, and said, patting the air with his hands, "Haven't any of you people ever seen a couple of boys fight before? It's a natural—"

"Natural?" Mrs. Frost yelled. "This—this *bully* never fought a boy his size in his life. He goes for smaller children always—"

Martin was getting very red, and Edward was feeling terribly ashamed of his mother, screaming that way. "Mom—" he began, but nobody heard him.

"I'd hardly call it an uneven fight," Mrs. Hastings said, thrusting her face at Mrs. Frost's, "when a mad dog is introduced on your child's side. I'm going to have the police on you, that's what I'm going to do."

"Mother!" Martin shouted. But nobody heard him either. Suddenly he bolted for the house.

"Edward," Uncle Josh said, "let's go in and clean you up, eh?"

Edward started off with him willingly enough, and just then Mr. Frost came pounding up the street. "What's going on here? I saw the crowd down the block, and I thought something awful had happened."

"Something awful *has* happened," said Mrs. Frost and Mrs. Hastings together, and in the crowd of bystanders there was a ripple of laughter.

Edward couldn't stand it any more. He marched toward the house, with Argess and Uncle Josh following, and went upstairs to the bathroom, where he took off his shirt and began to bathe his face. Uncle Josh got out some first-aid equipment.

"Maybe you ought to get in the tub," he said.

Edward shook his head. "Things are bad enough."

"Can't understand why you hate bathing so much," said Uncle Josh, gently blotting a scratch on Edward's neck. "Argess was doing her best, but she didn't precisely help."

"Sure she helped," said Edward in a muffled voice. "I hate taking baths because they *make* me."

"I see," said Uncle Josh, as if it were the most reasonable of explanations. "Still, under the present circumstances— Okay. Here, turn around. I have to put this on your scratches. It's going to sting."

Edward flinched, and endured. "She defended me," he said. "Did you see that?"

"I sure did. What was it all about, or don't you want to say?"

Edward hesitated. "I guess I don't, Uncle Josh."

"All right. Better get a clean shirt." He tipped his head. "There are your parents. Let's go down, shall we?" He paused. "Martin did put up a defense for Argess," he said tentatively.

"Oh, he's crazy about dogs," Edward said. Oddly enough, he found he wasn't feeling particularly angry at Martin any more. "He had one, once. But it got taken away from him."

"Why?"

"He didn't take care of it."

"Oh. Well, let's go down."

Mr. and Mrs. Frost were in the living room, Mrs. Frost in a furious silence, Mr. Frost in a thoughtful one.

"Well," he said to his son, "that was quite a mix-up, wasn't it?"

"Are you all right, Edward?" Mrs. Frost asked, coming to look him over. She touched his face gently. "Does it hurt?"

"Not much," said Edward, smiling at her. "As a matter of fact, I feel pretty good."

"Because you fought instead of running," said Mr. Frost. "It has its satisfactions."

"Savages, all of you," said Mrs. Frost.

"No," her husband said. "I don't think so, dear. Look at it this way . . . Edward's been running from this boy ever since he can remember. It's always good when the time comes that you face up to what frightens you. After that, it doesn't frighten you. You watch. Edward will be much better from now on."

"Yes, but will Martin? It's perfectly possible that Edward will be better and Martin will be worse, and then where are we? Wrestling over the lawns every afternoon, with me and that woman shrieking at each other like fishwives?" She shuddered a little. "I could just die."

"Oh, Mom," said Edward. "It wasn't that bad. You couldn't help it. You were angry." But he hoped that if he and Martin ever had to fight again, their mothers would be in a meeting at the other end of town. He also hoped he wouldn't have to fight Martin again, because if it hadn't been for Argess and all the people who appeared, he'd have lost. Badly. He was glad he'd lit into Martin for once, and he didn't see what else he could have done, but the truth was he didn't like fighting. He supposed some people did, but he didn't.

Mr. Frost got up. "There comes Hastings, into his driveway. I'm going over and see him."

"Oh, Ed," said Mrs. Frost. "What good will that do?"

"We can't just pretend nothing's happened. How do we know Martin's mother *won't* call the police about Argess?"

"She wouldn't dare. She'd have to admit that her son picks on babies."

"Listen, Mom," said Edward indignantly. "I'm not as big as Martin, but, my gosh, I'm not a pigmy. You act like he yanked me off a tricycle or something."

"Excuse me," said Mrs. Frost. "You know what I mean."

"Yeah, but still—"

"If I don't go over and try to make some sort of sense out of all this," Mr. Frost said, "next thing we know, we'll be building a spite fence. This has to be straightened out."

He was gone about fifteen minutes, and when he came back his face had a baffled expression.

"What happened?" said Mrs. Frost.

Her husband looked around the room a long time before he answered. Then he said, "He told me to go fry an egg, and I told him to go boil his head."

Mrs. Frost said, "*What?*" and Uncle Josh put his head back and roared.

Mr. Frost shrugged. "That's what happened. I guess we didn't get anywhere. Except they aren't going to call the police. I said if they did, I'd register a complaint against them for disturbing the peace."

"Oh, my word," said Mrs. Frost.

"When do we start building the spite fence?" said Uncle Josh.

CHAPTER

8

For a while life on Barkham Street was uneventful. Mrs. Frost and Mrs. Hastings passed in silence when they encountered each other. Mr. Frost ran for his bus every morning, trudged home from it each evening. The wrens had arranged the yellow house to their liking and were well settled in, and now in the big yard there were also brown thrashers, and flickers, and catbirds—those demure gray birds who sang so beautifully in the early morning and squawked the rest of the day. Uncle Josh could get catbirds to eat raisins from his hands.

"The trick," he explained to an envious Edward, "is to remain very still in one position for a long time. That way they either get to trust you or they decide you aren't alive. I haven't decided which."

"Well, if remaining very still in one position for a long time is the trick, you certainly have it made," said Mrs. Frost one day. She sounded a bit tart.

And even Edward, his great champion, had to admit that Uncle Josh was a trifle lazy.

Argess took to waking Edward in the morning and meeting him at the corner of Barkham and Elm every afternoon after school. This gave Edward an almost unbearable pleasure. He would lie very still in the morning, the sheet pulled over his head, and wait for the clatter of Argess' nails, and the tug at the sheet, and the lick of the pink tongue over his face. And he would pump up the hill from school, zigzagging back and forth, lifting his eyes now and then to see the light, sort of dancing figure of Argess at the top. Mrs. Frost decided that walking down the street to meet Edward didn't constitute running loose. She also decided that there was no reason for Argess to be barred from the living room, since she conducted herself so nicely when in it.

"You know, Edward," she said one day, for no apparent reason, "sometimes adults can be wrong about things."

Edward nodded. He thought it was nice of her to admit it. His mother was one of the few grown-ups he knew who ever did.

"I've been thinking," she went on, "about how I always insisted that you'd have to take the entire care of a dog by yourself. I suppose it was a way of trying to make you take the responsibility for *some*thing. But the more I think about it, the more I think there's no reason why if you did an honest part of the taking care, I shouldn't do some of it. When—" she hesitated, and sighed, and went on "—when Argess goes, that is."

"Goes?"

"Well, darling. Your Uncle Josh won't stay here forever. He never does stay anywhere very long. I thought you knew that. And, after all, Argess is his dog. We could—get you another one, I guess. If you wanted."

Edward's heart felt like a stone. He shook his head, unable to speak.

Still, the days passed, and Uncle Josh didn't leave, or talk of it. Argess continued to wake Edward in the morning, meet him in the afternoon, and he forgot, or put from his mind, any thought of ever being without her. But it was clear to Edward, if it wasn't to any of his family, that for him it was Argess or *no* dog.

Rod's brother-in-law left for Saudi Arabia, and his sister and his niece and his nephew moved in and Rod was relegated to the sewing room. Rod said he was going to have to lose twenty pounds in order to squeeze into the room and get to bed at all, and his mother got out the Poor Sportsmanship mask left over from the skit and tacked it to the sewing room door. This made Rod so angry that he had a fight with his sister and threw a carrot at her. ("Why a carrot?" Edward asked later. "It was what I had in my hand," Rod said. "Oh," said Edward. "Good thing it wasn't a baseball bat." Rod didn't answer.) This meant Rod had to be spanked by his father, and, though he admitted it was more humiliating than painful, Rod was madder than ever. Except when he was around Argess. With Argess, both boys forgot their troubles.

They spent a lot of time with Uncle Josh, listening to his tales of the West, so that after a while they almost felt that they had seen roundups, thick with dust and the bawling of driven cattle and the shrill whoops of cowboys, that they had wandered in a sun-white pueblo and seen the strings of blood-red chilies drying on adobe walls and talked with still-faced Navajos and heard their drums at night and the beat of bare feet dancing and the long, lifting chants. Edward could watch his wrens and think that he also knew the strange earthbound speed of a road runner and the swift dive of a water ouzel in a mountain stream.

Once in a while Uncle Josh fixed a leaky faucet

or ambled downtown on an errand for his sister, but generally he could be found lounging with his hands behind his head, his farseeing eyes fixed on something they could not see. Edward wondered if his uncle's dreaming eyes were seeing into what was past or what was ahead of him, but somehow he never asked. For all his easygoing ways, there were certain things you didn't ask Uncle Josh. And certain things he didn't answer, even if you did ask. Since the day of the fight they had never again mentioned Edward's hope that the two of them might travel together a little while in the summer. Uncle Josh didn't say anything, and Edward found he couldn't.

Martin was strangely quiet. Edward watched him as warily as ever, but Martin seemed to have forgotten his existence.

"You don't suppose he figures I was winning that day, do you?" Edward said to Rod. "He was just about to kill me when Argess moved in." He said this last with a pride that never subsided.

"Don't be a dope," Rod said. "He's got something up his sleeve."

"That's what I thought," said Edward, and he continued to watch Martin, who continued to ignore him.

And so time went on, and the leaves on the trees grew thicker, the days grew warmer and longer, lawns had to be mowed and sprinkled. It became harder and harder to go to school, and even Miss Hargraves occasionally looked out of the open classroom windows and fell into a dream.

Then a morning came when Edward waited in vain for the clattering nails, the tug, the eager tongue. He lay under the sheet till he was stifled. Then he pushed it away and sat up, waiting. He

wasn't allowing himself to think or be alarmed. He just waited.

And there was nothing. No sound of Argess belatedly on her way. No sound, he realized, of anything. He didn't hear his father's electric shaver, or his mother stirring about in the kitchen. He couldn't smell coffee. There wasn't a single thing to tell him it was morning, and yet—he looked at his clock to be sure—it was morning and time for everyone to be up and about. Time and way past for Argess to be here.

He got out of bed and moved into the hall in his bare feet. The door to Uncle Josh's room was closed and behind it all was quiet, so Argess couldn't be in there. He started for his parents' room, and then stopped to listen, because they were talking.

"How are we going to tell Edward?" his mother was saying. Her voice sounded tight and hurt.

"I don't know," Mr. Frost said. "I just don't know. Look, I don't understand this. He *can't* just have gone off, without a word, without an indication of where he was going or when he'd be back."

"He left that note."

"*Note,*" said Mr. Frost. "What kind of a note is that? *It's been great, see you again.* You call that a message?"

"No. No, it isn't. But it's as much as he's ever left behind him. That's all he left last time, and you weren't this upset."

"Last time he hadn't gotten Edward to love him. And he hadn't brought a dog that Edward—that everyone loves. This is different, don't you see?"

"I see. Only Josh didn't. That's what nobody but me ever understands about Josh. He *doesn't* see. He just does what he wants. Why do you suppose I almost never talk of him? Because he can't be relied on at all, and he hurts people. He broke Mother's heart, and Dad's, when he left the first time, and he's gone on leaving just the same way ever since."

"But he *loved* Edward," Mr. Frost said, sounding angry and baffled. "I'm sure he did."

"No," said Mrs. Frost. "He's fond of him. But Josh is fond of lots of people and lots of places. Nothing ever holds him."

Edward, leaning against the wall, his eyes closed, remembered that his mother had said eavesdroppers sometimes got hurt. He hadn't believed her. I don't think I'll eavesdrop any more, he said to himself. Not any more, after this. He started back to his room, hearing his father's voice saying, "Well, then, why did he have to take the *dog*?"

Edward sat down on his bed and hunched a little against the pain inside him. Uncle Josh, who hadn't loved him, was gone. And Argess, who probably had, was gone. He tried to hate his uncle, but somehow he couldn't even do that. As his mother said, Uncle Josh just was the way he was. He sat there, remembering what a nice man he'd been to talk to, how gentle, how quick to understand. He knew all about birds, and the Grand Canyon, and he didn't ask silly questions.

I'm going to miss Uncle Josh, he thought. And then, though he was trying not to think of Argess, he thought of her, and he leaned slowly over till his face was in the pillow.

A little while later he felt his mother's hand on his shoulder, and he turned around. Both his parents were in his room, and nobody seemed to know what to say.

"You were listening to us?" Mrs. Frost said at last.

Edward nodded.

"I'm sorry."

"Look, Edward," Mr. Frost said, "we'll get you a—" He stopped, lifted his shoulders, and looked around the room as if a solution might be written on the walls somewhere.

Mrs. Frost sat on the edge of the bed. "Maybe I'd better change one thing I said. What I meant, Edward, was that your Uncle Josh loves you—but in his own way. His way isn't like other people's."

Edward gulped, sniffled, and nodded. "I know. His way is—" He didn't know what Uncle Josh's way was.

"Irresponsible," said Mrs. Frost. "He can love, but he can't be depended on."

"Then the loving doesn't matter much, does it?" Edward burst out.

"I don't know," said his mother. "All love matters, I guess. It's just that with someone like Josh people have to take what he can give and not look for what he can't." She stood up. "Well, if you aren't both to be late, we'd better hurry." She hesitated, and looked at Edward. "I don't see anything else to do, do you?"

"No," Edward said dully. He got up. "I'll hurry, Mom."

Mr. Frost tousled his son's head and left the room without a word. A second later his electric shaver whirred, and Edward heard his mother going downstairs. He got into his clothes quickly, remembering, though he did not wish to, that yesterday Argess had taken one of his shoes and

147

dashed off with it, returning in a minute with one of his father's in its place. She had taken a peculiar pleasure in transposing their belongings, and not even Uncle Josh, who understood animals pretty well, had been able to figure out why. Edward shook his head and wondered why you couldn't make your mind stop thinking of things you didn't want to think of.

Breakfast was hurried, with spurts of conversation that led nowhere. Mrs. Frost said she was going to shop this morning, and Mr. Frost said, "Fine," just as Edward said, "That's too bad." There was a little laugh, and silence. Mr. Frost said the chancellor of the university was going to Europe in the summer, and Mrs. Frost said how nice for him. Edward said Rod's brother-in-law had written it was hot in Saudi Arabia. "What could he expect?" said Mr. Frost, standing up. He took his brief case, kissed his wife, gave Edward a perplexed look, and said, "Try to—" He stopped.

"Yeah, I know, Dad," Edward said, and then, as he always did, "Have a good day."

"Oh, sure," said Mr. Frost. "Sure thing." He ran.

Edward got up. "I better be going too, Mom."

"Edward?"

"Yes, Mom?"

"Please don't take your bike. You'll be absent-minded."

"I won't."

He walked slowly along Barkham Street in the morning sun, wondering if he'd even bother to stop at Rod's, when Mike Toomy ran up beside him, and said, "Hey, Edward. Wait up. I gotta tell you something."

"Hi, Mike," Edward said in a dull voice. He stopped and waited for what Mike had to tell him.

"You already heard?" Mike asked.

"Heard what?" Edward asked indifferently.

"About Martin. I mean, what he said. You sound funny."

"I feel funny. What did dopey Martin say?"

"Well, somebody told me he said he was gonna be laying for you this afternoon after school with a bunch of guys from the sixth grade."

A moment ago, Edward would have said that nothing anyone told him would affect him one way or another, but now, in spite of his hurt and his inability to believe that Uncle Josh had really done this thing, he felt a stir of uneasy interest in what Mike was saying.

"Why?" he said, to mark time.

"Oh, it's all over school that you licked Martin

in a fight. I guess he doesn't like the idea of people saying somebody smaller than him beat him up."

"I didn't beat him up," Edward said, and he felt again that clutching sort of pain as he remembered Argess hurling herself into the fray, scratching him and Martin both, but undoubtedly defending Edward. "I didn't anything like beat him up."

"But that's what everybody's saying. And I heard Martin's madder than hops, so that's what he's going to do."

"A bunch of sixth-grade guys all against me?" Edward said. He ran his tongue over dry lips.

"That's what I heard. So what I thought is, let's get *all* the fifth-grade guys, and show him. Them."

"All of them could beat all of us."

"Martin can't get *all* of them to fight for him," Mike said scornfully. "I don't know how he got any."

"Where are we gonna have this fight?" said Edward, unable to take Mike's spirited view of the situation.

"I don't know. I just heard he's gonna be laying for you. Some place."

Edward caught his breath. The idea of all those guys waiting for him some place was awful. He didn't think Martin could get all the sixth grade to fight for him, but he didn't think, either, that the entire body of fifth-grade boys would go against them. For one thing, everybody was busy after school, with ballgames and music lessons and things. They'd just disappear, unless Martin and his gang showed up to fight in the schoolyard, and Edward knew they wouldn't do that. They'd just be . . . *some* place.

"What are you gonna do?" Mike asked.

"I don't know," Edward said. They walked on slowly. "I'm going over to Rod's now. You want to come?"

"I gotta get down to school and finish that spelling paper before class, because I gotta leave at one-thirty today. My mother's calling for me. We're going away for the weekend to my grandparents' golden wedding anniversary."

"I thought you were gonna help me fight?"

Mike looked stricken. "I forgot," he said, and added heartily, "Well, everybody else would, I suppose. I couldn't miss my grandparents' golden wedding anniversary, could I? Even if I'd be let, and I wouldn't."

Edward wasn't at all interested in Mike's grandparents' golden wedding anniversary. He turned the corner of Rod's street without even saying good-by.

Rod was waiting for him on the sidewalk, in a

state of furious impatience. "Where have you been?" he demanded. "I've been waiting for hours."

Edward shrugged. "I'm here."

"What's the matter with you?"

"Plenty."

"Well, there's plenty the matter with me, too. Listen, Edward, let's get away from here. Come *on*." He tugged at Edward's shirt sleeve, and they started down the street toward school. "There's the first bell."

"So what," said Edward, "I don't care if I get to school or not."

He was a bit surprised at having said the words, but realized all at once that they were true. He not only didn't care, he positively didn't want to go at all. There'd be Martin and his gang to worry about all day. And in the afternoon, when he looked up Elm toward Barkham, there'd be no Argess waiting there to greet him. Not today, and never again. He frowned and trudged along, his feet dragging, his heart dragging. He felt as if his whole life had somehow dragged to a standstill, and he hardly heard what Rod was saying.

"Are you listening to me?" Rod said loudly.

"Yeah. No. Start over again and I'll listen this time."

"*Crums*. . . .You're as bad as my folks. I can't get anybody to listen to me about anything any more."

"What were you saying? I said I'd listen."

"What I was saying was nobody listens to me any more. I can't *get* anyone to listen. I've been asking my mother for a week to make me a pecan pie, and all she ever says is be sure I don't wake the baby up. Wake it up! It keeps me awake the whole night long. It's a colicky baby. Do you know what that means?" Edward shook his head. "It means," Rod went on angrily, "that it cries and yells all the time and if you do ever get it to sleep you gotta slip around like you didn't have any feet so it won't wake up and start yelling again. And do you know what happened last night? I went *up* to this teeny room they've got me stashed away in and I put on my radio. I gotta have *some*thing, don't I? If nobody's going to listen to me or talk to me, I at least can play my radio, can't I?"

"Are you *asking* me?"

"No. Just listen. That's all I'm asking you. So I went up and put on my radio, and it sort of blared just at first. You know. You can't always tell how loud it's going to be when you just put it on. So it blared. So you know what happened?"

"Sure. The baby was asleep and it woke up."

"And I got walloped."

"You did?" In spite of his troubles, Edward managed to feel indignant for Rod. "That wasn't fair."

"That's what I told them. I told them the baby kept me awake all the time, so why couldn't I keep it awake sometime. And I told my mother I didn't care if she ever baked another pecan pie in her whole life. And I told my sister I wished she and her kids were somewhere in Iceland. And I told my father I didn't care if he walloped me till I dropped dead."

"He doesn't hit you that hard."

"Oh, I told them, all right," Rod said with gloomy satisfaction. "I certainly told them."

"Sounds like it." The tardy bell rang, and they were still half a block from school. "So then what happened?"

"Oh . . . they sent me up to my room, and I can't play the radio till I'm sixty-five or something, and this morning my father said was I prepared with an apology to everybody, and I said no, I wasn't."

"Then what did he say?" Edward asked, his interest now thoroughly caught.

"He said he'd see me tonight."

There was silence, and then Edward said, "That's tough."

Rod nodded.

They were at the school gates, turning in, when Edward suddenly stopped. "I'm not going to school, Rod."

"What?"

"You heard me."

"Oh, for Pete's sake, Edward. We'll get in more trouble than we're already in." He scratched his head. "Are you in trouble? I mean, what's with you that you won't go to school? I can see me—except I'd make things worse than ever, but—"

Edward had thought he wouldn't be able to mention Uncle Josh or Argess, but now he burst out, feeling that terrible pain again in his chest, his throat, "Uncle Josh took off last night, just like that. He's just gone."

"Gone where?"

"He didn't say. Gone, like he always goes. A wanderer," Edward said bitterly. "Wanderers don't tell people what they're doing, apparently."

"Well, what about—" Rod began, and stopped, biting his lip.

"She's gone with him," Edward said. He kicked at the gate with his foot. "And Martin's gonna lay for me with a bunch of sixth-graders after school, Mike says."

The two boys looked at each other with a sense of everything lost and laid waste. They were already so late for school that they'd have to go to the principal's office and explain before they could even get in class. No reasonable explanation occurred to them. So that would be more trouble. There was trouble behind them, and, as far as they could see, little but trouble ahead.

"Come on, Edward," Rod said suddenly, "let's beat it."

They ran, expecting any second that a late-arriving teacher would spot them and call out, or a policeman would ask what they were doing at this hour and find out. They cut in the park without interference, and ran till they were panting. At a grove where, on weekends or in the summer, people picnicked, they dropped to the ground, gasping and astounded. Now there was no one here but themselves. Squirrels ran over the wooden picnic tables and benches, a bluejay leaned over a branch and scolded them. They could hear traffic in the distance, and, to the other side of them, the sound of a train coupling in the freight yards.

Since they had no idea of what they were going to do next, for a long time they said nothing. Edward lay on his back and thought about Uncle Josh's stories of bobcats and mountain trails and black bears and the people you met and parted from when you wandered, and how sometimes you were hungry and sometimes cold but you kept wandering, if that was what you were meant to do. He wondered where they were now, Uncle Josh and Argess. He tried to picture them, walking along together on a road some place. Wouldn't they be missing him, and his parents? Wouldn't they be *sorry?* He wondered if he'd ever be able to breathe again without hurting.

I guess, he said to himself, he never did mean to take me with him this summer.

"This is sort of fun, hey?" said Rod.

"What is?"

"Oh . . . being here, like this. They're all back in that classroom studying, and here we are."

Edward sat up. "Wonder what they're doing now?"

"Geography, I suppose. I suppose it's still pretty early."

Neither of them had a watch.

"Let's walk over to the freight yards," Edward said.

"Okay," Rod said dubiously. "We aren't supposed to."

"We aren't supposed to be doing anything we're doing."

They walked through the park, across a bridge, and down to the yards, expecting always that someone would stop them. No one did. They wandered along a spur track, reading the names of the cars. The Delaware and Lackawanna. The Lakeland Route. The Santa Fe Trail. They walked on, to where a long freight was idling on a main track. A man in a striped coverall and a railroader's cap came toward them and they stiffened, waiting to be questioned. But he said, "Morning, boys," in an incurious voice and went past.

"Maybe he thinks it's a holiday, or something," Rod decided.

"Maybe he doesn't care," Edward said.

They were beside a car of which the wide middle doors were open, and they stopped and looked at it, and then at each other.

"Want to get in?" Edward asked.

Rod hesitated. "Might as well," he said finally. They just managed to scramble on, but once

there they became suddenly exhilarated, and ran about the empty car heedless of any noise they made. They stood at the tremendous square of the open door and gazed about imperiously. They were only a few feet above the ground, but somehow the great, empty length of the car, the tremendous latent power of the freight stretching to either side of them gave them a sense of control.

"Everything's in my iron sway," Edward said loudly, sweeping his arms about. "I am the KING!"

"And I am the King's Immediate Superior," said Rod, with a great leap into the car's interior. Edward ran after him, protesting that this was impossible.

"Nothing's impossible," said Rod. "I am MERLIN, the Possible Maker!"

They beat each other on the back and laughed, and sank down in a shadowed corner of the car, stretching their legs out before them.

"I'm a magnate," said Edward, tapping on an imaginary cigar. "This is my private magnate's railroad car." He summoned an invisible servant. "Mag me something, varlet!"

"I've just robbed the biggest mail train in the whole Southwest," said Rod. "I'm sitting here on a bag of gold and diamonds."

"I'd rather sit on my velvet magnate's armchair," Edward said.

"Ssh," said Rod, grabbing his arm.

"What's the matter?"

"There's somebody out there. Keep still."

Holding their breath, they waited in the dark corner of the empty car and wondered what would happen if they were discovered.

"Wait'll they go away," Rod whispered. "Then we'll get out of here."

It came over Edward in a flash that once again he and Rod were behaving in an irresponsible fashion, and he felt pretty discouraged. In one way, with Argess gone, it didn't seem to matter much, but in another he was awfully sorry. His parents felt pretty nearly as bad as he did about Uncle Josh and Argess. And now they'd have to feel bad about their son, too.

Suddenly, Rod's hand tightened on his arm, and he said hoarsely, "*Edward* . . . they're closing the door!"

It was true. A man had glanced in casually, had failed to see them in the shadows, and now the big door was sliding shut. Edward jumped to his feet and ran in the blackness, stumbling once, to where he knew the door was. He shouted, "Hey, we're in here! Let us out!"

"Do you think we better say anything?" Rod asked anxiously. "I mean, we aren't supposed—"

Edward was beating on the door. "I don't want to go with this thing," he said almost sobbing. "Help me yell, Rod."

Rod lifted his voice and howled. He kicked at the door, and shouted with Edward, "Hey, out there! *We're in here.*"

But the door didn't budge, and no one came, and in a second they felt the shudder of the train in motion, the slow turn of the wheels picking up speed little by little, clicking, clicking. They beat on the door and yelled long after they knew it was of no use at all, and then they leaned against it, shaken and scared. Slowly they sank to the floor and for what seemed hours couldn't exchange a word.

The train shook and rattled and raced on. Now and again the diesel horn wailed above them. There was no sign of slackening. In the dark, Edward and Rod, leaning against each other for comfort, stared into the blackness. There were chinks here and there through which daylight shone, but not enough to give them any real light to move around by. And where would they move to?

On and on, with the horn braying like a lonely animal and the wheels clicking beneath them, the car swaying as it rounded corners and vibrating in a way that made their heads teeter.

"Where do you suppose we're going?" Rod said at last in a tense voice.

"I dunno," Edward whispered. "Could be anywhere."

"But when do you suppose it'll stop?"

"I don't *know*. How would I know?"

"No point getting mad at me," Rod said limply. "Gee, I wish we hadn't gotten on."

"I wish we hadn't, too."

Then again there was a long silence. Edward was remembering that once some kids had gotten in a freight car like this and the car hadn't been opened for weeks or something. It got put on a siding and left. The kids had died. Edward swallowed hard. He was feeling quite sick, and wondering whether to mention those other kids to Rod.

"Well, it's gotta stop sometime," Rod said. "They'll want to load it, or something. Then we can get out. Boy, we're gonna catch it this time."

Edward decided to say nothing about sidings and the fact that they might never be in a position again *to* catch it. I wouldn't mind what they did,

163

he thought faintly. Just so we could get out of here.

"I wonder what time it is," Rod said.

"Late, I guess. What will they do when they miss us? I mean, I should think they'd track us down somehow."

"How? It may be ages before they even know we're gone."

"What do you mean? They know we aren't in school right now."

"Yeah, but who's to say it isn't because we're with our folks somewhere? The school doesn't call to ask why you're out. Not the first day." Rod was breathing heavily. "You know what, Edward? They're gonna think we ran away. My folks will think it's because of Dad being mad at me, and Toomy will tell how Martin was laying for you—"

"Toomy's gonna be gone for a few days. He won't even know about it. His grandparents are having their golden wedding anniversary."

"That's nice," Rod said politely.

It made them laugh, and for a little while they felt better. After all, the train would probably stop somewhere. The worst that could happen was that their parents would be terribly angry, and that seemed like nothing compared to this.

Then Edward said, "They're gonna be awful scared."

"Who?"

"Our families."

"Yeah. I guess they are. *Gee,* I'm sorry we got on this thing."

Edward was beginning to ache all over. He shifted his position, but it didn't help much. Beside him, he could feel Rod trembling, only of course that could be from the motion of the train. He wished they had a flashlight. It would just be dumb to say so, but he went on wishing it in silence. It made as much sense, anyway, as for Rod to go on wishing they hadn't climbed on this thing in the first place.

They lost all sense of time and all desire to talk. The train hurtled on and on, and the two boys sat together in the swaying darkness, wondering where they were going, and what was going to happen to them.

CHAPTER
9

In a small town some three hours by rail north of St. Louis a baggage man was walking beside a line of freights that had made an unscheduled stop due to a truck stalled on the tracks. He'd had a little talk with the engineer, who was enraged, and had left him because so much bad humor on such a pleasant day was disagreeable.

Since neither the freight nor the truck nor the engineer's plight was any concern of his, the baggage man was whistling to himself. His heavy boots scuffed the cinders. The roar of a passenger train on a far track swept the air and then diminished around a curve.

The baggage man stopped suddenly, thinking he'd heard another sound, a thudding accompanied by faint yells. He was just about to decide it was imagination when he heard it again and turned his head curiously. There was something, all right, that was not part of the usual noises in a trainman's day. He retraced his steps, keeping his head cocked.

Then, with an abrupt rush, he made for an empty refrigerator car that was part of the stalled freight. The door was closed but unlocked. He pushed it open and stood for a moment shocked speechless, and also frightened. It had been only chance that led him here, and it might have been days before this particular car was opened for any reason at all, and here in it were two boys. White-faced, grimy, shoes in hand, they stood unsteadily, blinking down at him.

The trainman swallowed heavily, muttered something under his breath, and held up his arms to help down one boy and then the other, when he stood glaring at them and finally shouted, "What the devil do you boys think you're doing?"

One of them shook his head, the other said, "Thank you," in a shaky voice, and then they stood looking up at him, waiting.

The baggage man shoved his cap to the back of his head and said, "I yelled because you had me scared." They nodded. "I guess you're pretty scared yourselves," he added, and they nodded again. "Well, put on your shoes, boys. We'll see what's to do about you. I hope you get your voices back pretty soon."

"I'm Edward Frost, sir," said one of the boys, "and this is my friend, Rod Graham."

"Under the circumstances," said the baggage man, "I can hardly say I'm pleased to meet you. But I'm glad to know who you are. Where do you come from?"

"From near St. Louis," said Rod. He finished tying his shoes and stood up. "What day is it, sir?"

"Friday."

"Friday?" The two boys looked at each other. "You mean it's still today?"

"Friday, a little past noon." The man looked at them sympathetically. "I guess you thought it was a good deal later?"

"We thought we'd been in there for days," said Edward weakly. He felt a little lift of hope. "Crums, Rod. I bet nobody even knows we're gone yet."

"Well, don't think they aren't going to," said the baggage man firmly. "This isn't just a kid's joke, you know. Do you realize you might not have got out of there in—in time?"

Edward and Rod looked at him and nodded again. It was serious all right, and they saw that there wasn't a chance of simply going back home somehow and keeping quiet about it. They went with the baggage man, who held each of them by an arm—whether for support or to keep them from running away, Edward wasn't sure—to the station and the ticket master's office. It was quite small. There was one man at a switchboard with earphones, and another at the ticket window. They both looked around when the baggage man and the boys entered.

Edward and Rod braced themselves for some pretty narrow questioning, and it came. Like the baggage man, these two men got angry at first when they heard where the boys had been found, and then apologized for yelling, and then asked if they understood what might have happened.

Edward thought of the long, black, terrified hours and shuddered. It almost felt as if they were back there, beating on the door with their shoes and yelling hoarsely and thinking no one would ever hear or come, thinking they'd never see daylight or home again, but trying not to think what that really meant.

Still, somebody *had* come and here they were, and he wished these men would stop pointing out what a narrow escape they'd had. He and Rod knew, and there wasn't a chance they'd ever forget. If there was one thing about grownups that drove Edward crazy, it was the way they repeated. They never thought you'd heard anything until they said it six times.

He and Rod agreed several times that they did understand, and explained how sorry they were, but Edward kept thinking that now they were out of the car there wasn't much point in going on about what would have happened if they hadn't gotten out. He was more inclined to worry about what was coming next. Leaning back on a bench, tired, and beginning to get hungry, he wondered how they were going to get home and what to say when they got there.

"What did you run away for?" the switchboard man said.

Rod, who was in the middle of a yawn, stopped and said, "We didn't."

"You didn't? You weren't taking the half-day excursion in that refrigerator car."

"We got in it by mistake. I mean, we were just hacking around."

"Why weren't you hacking around in school?"

Rod didn't answer, and Edward, who was starting to dislike the switchboard man, said, "We had

a reason. We had a lot of reasons."

"What were they?"

Edward clamped his mouth shut, and without consulting each other he and Rod agreed not to answer any more of the switchboard man's questions. In a little while it became clear to the men in the ticket office that this was the case, and the baggage man said, "Go easy, Bud. They've had a scare."

"I think we should call the cops," said the switchboard man. "They're the ones to deal with runaways."

Rod stiffened, and Edward thought about hamburgers so as not to hear the switchboard man at all. Except for the baggage man, he thought the police would be an improvement. In all the stories he'd ever heard, at least the police fed you if you were lost, or had run away. Not that he and Rod had, but it was bound to look peculiar, the way they'd wound up in this town that they didn't even know the name of when they were supposed to be safe at school.

He fell into a sort of daze, in which all voices and sounds became a thick distant hum, and started up nervously when a new voice said, "Okay, son. Wake up now." Lifting his head heavily he stared at Rod, and then at a young policeman that Rod was standing beside.

"Wake up?" he said in confusion. "Oh. Oh, sure. What're we gonna do now?"

"We'll take a ride over to the station and see about getting you boys back home. Come along."

Edward got to his feet, yawned enormously, started to stumble after the policeman. At the door, he turned. The switchboard man had the earphones on and his back to them. The ticket man waved and said, "Good luck."

"Where's the baggage man?" Edward asked.

"He left a while ago. Had to unload some mail."

"Will you say thank you to him for us?"

"Sure thing."

Edward and Rod hesitated. They felt somehow that they owed the baggage man something more.

But the policeman urged them gently along and into a waiting squad car. When Rod explained that the baggage man had probably saved their lives, the policeman agreed but said it was over now, and the baggage man wouldn't want thanks, he'd just be glad he'd been there.

Edward was next to the window, with Rod between him and the policeman, and he was trying hard to take some pleasure in this ride. He'd never ridden in a police car before, and he'd always wanted to. He'd always thought that if you rode in a police car people would look at you and wonder and you'd be pretty much the center of attention. But now his eyes kept falling shut and swift strange notions fled across his brain—mostly that he and Rod were back in the dark, musty-smelling refrigerator car and that no one was ever going to let them out. He'd jerk his lids up and stare, making himself know they were out and safe, and then down they'd go again and the reality would fuzz away and they'd be back there pounding on the great closed door and neither of them daring to cry. . . .

The policemen bought them hamburgers and milk and chocolate bars, and, while they ate, asked them questions. It was mostly Rod who answered.

". . . so, you see," Rod explained, "we didn't really run away. We more got taken away, like."

"I guess," said Sergeant Young, who was at the desk, "you realize now that you shouldn't have gotten in that freight car. You won't do it again, will you?"

"Oh gosh, no," said Rod. Even Edward found his voice long enough to deny any wish, intention, or will ever to get into another freight car. "I don't think I want to get on any sort of a train again," Rod said, peeling the wrapper from his chocolate bar.

"Well," said the sergeant, "I haven't been able to get anyone at either of your houses. I'd think there'd be someone at yours, Rod, with all those babies you say drove you to this life of crime."

Rod laughed patiently, but Edward didn't bother. He was in no mood to humor grownups about what they thought was funny. He was too tired.

Rod explained that probably his mother and sister and the babies were at the pediatrician's.

"They said this morning they were going, so I guess they went."

"I see," said the sergeant. He looked closely at Edward. "If you boys don't mind sleeping in a cell, we can give you a couple of cots to stretch out on. No other prisoners today, so you'll have the place to yourselves."

This time Edward managed a smile. After all, the sergeant and the other policeman were being very nice, and it was funny, being invited to sleep in a jail.

"I'll keep calling your homes," the sergeant called after them as they trudged in the footsteps of the young policeman who'd come to the station. "You just have a rest."

Two minutes later Rod and Edward were asleep on the thin hard bunks of the jail of a town that they still didn't know the name of.

When Edward woke, daylight had gone gray and a church bell was striking five. He lay for a minute or two, puzzled and faintly frightened, before he remembered where he was, and why. He twisted around to look at the bunk above him, then got up and saw that Rod was gone. Stepping to the door of the cell, he heard voices to the right and went in search of them. He ran right into his mother.

"Oh, Edward," she said, putting her arms around him. "Edward, what in the *world* happened?"

Edward rubbed his eyes and, just for a moment, leaned against her. Then he stood away and said, "It was a mistake, Mom." She looked so unhappy that he added, "You'll see. I'm gonna behave better." He hoped he was going to. Anyway, he could try for a while.

On the long drive home nobody talked very much. In spite of their sleep, Edward and Rod weren't feeling lively, and Mrs. Frost drove with a little frown of concentration. Edward decided not to wonder what she was concentrating on. There were times, and today was one of them, when the whole world of adults threatened to overwhelm him, and the only escape was to ignore them, even the nice ones, like his mother, or Sergeant Young, or the baggage man.

Once Rod said, "Are my folks awful mad, Mrs. Frost?"

She shook her head. "Not angry. Frightened, upset." She took a deep breath. "Your mother said to tell you she's making you a pecan pie."

Rod turned this over in his mind. "That's funny," he said at last. "She wouldn't make me one when I was staying home where I belonged."

"Oh, try to understand, won't you? We can get pretty angry at everyday things. And you know why. We're trying to bring you up, bring you up properly. But when something like this happens, we're too terrified to be angry. Too grateful that you're safe, I suppose."

"I guess I see," Rod mumbled, and Edward, as he did every once in a while, felt vaguely sorry for parents.

Night fell. Towns they had passed were lit up, and the highway itself became a steady stream of headlights. Edward thought back to this morning, and it seemed a week away. He wondered where Uncle Josh and Argess were now. On a night like this, would they sleep out? Or would Uncle Josh find some barn, or pay for a cheap motel?

I don't see why they had to leave like that, he said to himself. I won't ever understand.

Mrs. Graham was waiting at the window when they pulled into Rod's driveway. She rushed out and grabbed Rod, who'd clambered out of the car. She and Mrs. Frost said something to each other that Edward didn't listen to, and then the car was in motion again, and finally they were home.

Standing on the front porch steps were his father, and Uncle Josh, and Argess.

Argess made a dive for Edward, who threw his arms around her and shook her back and forth and laughed because she was licking his face so hard he couldn't see.

Mrs. Frost remained for some time on the walk, staring at her brother. Finally she said, "What are you doing here?" Edward wanted to protest at the tone of her voice, but decided he had better not.

"Wasn't my idea," said Uncle Josh easily. "It was Argess, here. She wouldn't go with me. Kept turning around and heading back, so I thought I better come along and make sure she got here. If you'll keep her, of course. I know you never bargained to have a dog for good."

"We'll keep her," said Mr. Frost, as if there could be no question. Edward looked at his mother, who nodded. He buried his face in the fur of Argess' neck and wondered if it was really possible to burst with happiness.

"Well," said Mr. Frost, "there's no point in standing out here all night. Let's go inside. You hungry, Edward?"

Edward nodded. Hungry, happy, sleepy. He felt fine.

"I'll come in for a bit," said Uncle Josh. "Find out what's been going on here."

"For a bit?" said Mrs. Frost, as they went into the kitchen. "You can't mean you're leaving again *tonight*?"

"Yup."

"But you can't go at this hour."

"Sure can. I only want to find out if Edward ran away because of . . . of my leaving so unceremoniously. Not that I can see what to do about it if he did. Except be sorry. Darned sorry."

"I didn't run away, Uncle Josh," Edward said.

"What did happen?" his father asked.

Once again Edward explained, while his mother fixed him supper and Argess sat beside him.

"So that was it," said Uncle Josh when he'd finished. "A chain of circumstances. Me, Argess, Martin, and Rod's niece and nephew. . . . By the way, Edward, your father had a talk with Martin this evening."

"Yeah?" said Edward curiously. "How come?" he asked his father.

"Your friend Mike Toomy told Miss Hargraves about Martin's threats, when you didn't come to class, and Miss Hargraves told your mother, and your mother phoned me before she left to pick you up. So when I got home I went over and had a talk with Martin. Fortunately his parents were out."

"What did you say?"

"Martin said he didn't mean it. He just wanted to scare you."

"Oh, he scares me all right," Edward admitted, patting Argess' head. "What did you say?"

"Well, I'll tell you, Edward. I told Martin that I wanted to talk to a part of him I knew was there . . . the part that's a good sport."

"Huh," said Edward.

"Keep on with that attitude, and you'll undo whatever good I've done." Edward said nothing, and his father went on. "Whether you'll admit it or not, in some ways Martin is a good sport. I've seen enough to know. The way he conducted himself that night of the skit. The way he stuck up for Argess when you had the fight. The way he reacted tonight. I told him that, leaving his parents out of it, and us as a family out of it, did the part of him that was a good sport approve of the way he bullies younger children. He finally said he thought not. I think he really saw the point, and I think he'll try to do better. But I'll tell you something else, Edward. You sit there looking so innocent, and you always sound so innocent when one of these fracases occurs, but you needle that boy, you and your friends. So I want you to stop calling him Fatso, and—well, whatever else it is you do that gets him so furious."

We don't do anything, Edward thought, until he's already furious and beating up on us or breaking our things or calling *us* names. Fatso isn't any worse than Weird One. But he decided not to say anything. There was no point in getting his father on Martin's side altogether, and maybe there was a chance that talking with a grownup who called him a good sport instead of hollering at him all the time the way his own parents did would make Martin nicer. It seemed a long chance, but it was worth trying.

"Well then, that's that," said Uncle Josh, getting up. "I'll be off."

Mrs. Frost stared at him in indignation and surprise. "You mean you're leaving just like that? No explanation, no . . . no apology, or anything?"

"Afraid so," said Uncle Josh. He looked around at them and smiled. "Well, one small apology. I'm a little bit sorry to be the way I am. Just a mite. But it can't be changed at this point in my life."

Edward could not help admiring him. He didn't ask questions, and he didn't make explanations, and he did what he wanted to do. Still, along with his admiration, Edward also couldn't help realizing that he no longer wanted to grow up to be like Uncle Josh, that no one could ever depend on, and who didn't really care about anybody. Not even Argess.

A peculiar man, his Uncle Josh. Edward supposed that maybe he was one of the most peculiar men in the world.

"Where are you going?" Mrs. Frost asked.

"Well—I think I'm going to Arabia."

"When are you coming back?" Edward asked.

Uncle Josh pondered, lifted his shoulders. "Don't know. Oh, I meant to tell you, Edward, that that dog of Ulysses' never went traveling with him at all. Argus earned distinction by recognizing Ulysses when the old boy turned up after a twenty-year absence. I hope Argess will recognize me when I get back. It won't be twenty years."

Edward started to ask what about that trip they had been going to take together this summer, and then decided he didn't want to take it. Uncle Josh might get absent-minded and just leave him at the bottom of the Grand Canyon, or something, the way the man had left Argess. Uncle Josh was very absent-minded. Maybe, Edward thought, I can talk Mom and Dad into going to the Grand Canyon this summer. It would be safer that way. Edward thought he'd had enough of risks to last a long time.

They went with Uncle Josh to the front door and stood watching while he walked away under the street lamps, through the leafy shadows, into the dark. When he was gone, Mr. Frost closed the door and they went back in the house together in silence.

Mrs. Frost sat down in her chair, but made no move to pick up her book. Mr. Frost settled at the desk, but did not pick up his papers. Edward looked at the television, but didn't turn it on.

Suddenly, to everyone's surprise, Edward said, "I think I'll take a bath."

He whistled to his dog and they went upstairs together.

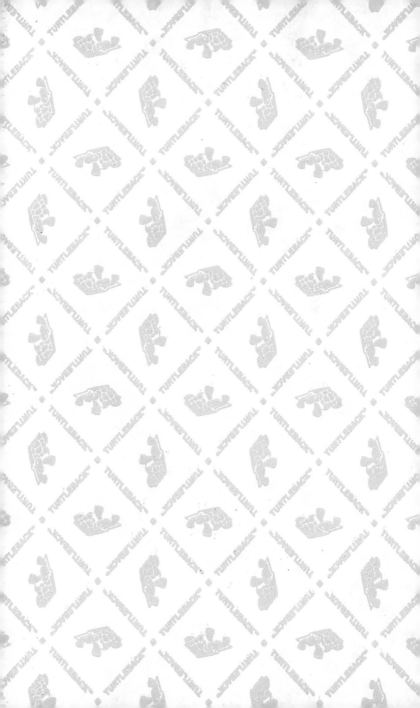